# A MURDER FOR CHRISTMAS

P.C. JAMES

# FAMILY MATTERS – DECEMBER 21, 1962

## NORTH RIDING OF YORKSHIRE 1962

"YOU HAVE TO, SIS," Alan said, "I said you would."

"Why did you do that?" Pauline said angrily. Alan was the last word in obnoxious older brothers. Even as a kid, he was forever getting his younger siblings in trouble with one lunatic scheme after another. Weren't the older kids supposed to be more mature than the younger ones? Pauline was sure there was a popular expression to that effect.

"It will be easy for you," Alan said. "Look at how you're always solving murders and such for the police. This is simple compared to that. Some small local disturbances are all we're asking you to solve. It will take you a matter of hours. It won't even disturb your holiday."

Her holiday. Two weeks with Mum and Dad on the farm over a cold and increasingly snowy Christmas, with Mum ill and Dad laid up. Some holiday! Now this idiot, her blasted brother, had promised her time looking into silly pranks in his village five miles away. With the roads the way they were and the weather the way it was, how could she do that without moving in with Alan and his wife, Bessie?

"I'm not doing it, Alan. Mum and dad need me here, not over at Goathland, chasing naughty children."

"Me and Jim will come to the farm every day to look after the beasts," Alan said, "and you'll have it all sorted out in a day, likely."

This was ridiculous. She'd driven down to her family home only the night before, straight after work, taking this Saturday morning off work to be here earlier. It had been a frightening journey with snow on the roads here in the Dales. On the high ground, a wicked wind swirled the snow in the headlamps, blinding her view through the icy windscreen. And there'd been few other cars on the road after she'd left the main highway. Now, next morning, when she was barely recovered from her fright, Alan arrives at the farm demanding she leave and solve mysterious events in the village and farms around him.

"No," Pauline said. "You people live there; it will be your children doing this. You local folk sort it out yourselves."

"It's not the children, Polly," Alan said, lapsing into the family nickname Pauline hated. "We thought that too at first. But it isn't. It's something bigger than it seems."

"In Goathland! What could be *big* in any way in Goathland?"

As she followed him back to his farm, however, she remembered what could be bigger. She couldn't miss it, or to be precise, them. Stark opal white against low black clouds that threatened yet more snow, the giant 'golf balls' of the Fylingdales early warning station loomed menacingly over moor and dale. Placed there by the United States Air Force and operated by the Royal Air Force, they were supposed to give the West fifteen minutes warning should the Soviet Union launch its intercontinental nuclear ballistic missiles, or so it was said. No one knew for sure. They were too secret for real knowledge. Pauline frowned as she tried to keep her eyes on the road and away from the golf balls. Her first investigation (she never said 'case' it was too official-sounding) had

2

been about spies, though she hadn't realized that until the very end. Was this about spies too and should she be thinking about them from the very beginning?

After saying hello to Alan's wife, Bessie, and the children, Alan said, "We're going straight to the manor house."

"Why?" Pauline asked, bewildered. The family at the manor hadn't been mentioned in Alan's earlier list of odd incidents.

"Because they have a story to tell I think you should hear."

Leaving her own car in the yard of Alan's farm, Pauline climbed into his Land Rover and they set off back up the farm road to the country lane that connected the farms along this dale with the outside world.

"What's this all about, Alan?" Pauline asked, as she pulled her coat, scarf, and collar closer around her. The Land Rover's heating was making no impression on the air temperature inside the cab, not that Alan seemed to notice. She wished she offered to drive in her own comfortable Wolseley, with its better seats and heating.

"Mr. Thornton will explain," he said.

"What has it to do with the incidents you told me about?"

"Not sure. Maybe nothing. I think it does but you'll have to decide for yourself."

Pauline gritted her teeth and stared out of the window. The afternoon looked like it promised more snow by the time they were returning home. Maybe the Land Rover with its four-wheel drive was the better choice for this journey. As it bumped over the frozen, rutted farm road, however, jarring every bone in her body, she found that little comfort. And imagining the drive back to her parents' farm through snow-covered roads in her own car gave her the shudders.

At the manor, an old-fashioned stone-built house that hadn't been upgraded in any of the architectural styles of the past four hundred years (and was all the better for it, in Pauline's opinion) she met Frank Thornton, the soon-to-be lord of the manor. Or at least that was what had been expected until the family solicitor had hurried up to the manor on the death of Frank's father only two days ago with some disastrous news.

"So, you see, Miss Riddell," Frank Thornton said, "we're in a pickle."

"Let me get this clear in my mind," Pauline said. "Your father has been training you up to take over the estate all your life. He never suggested any other course of action was being considered?"

"That's correct."

"The will has been lodged with the family solicitors for decades, since your older brother was killed in World War II, in fact? No one else has had access to it?" Pauline asked, with growing incredulity.

"That's correct," Thornton agreed.

"And the will, so far as everyone understood, named you as the heir to the estate and your younger brother, Anthony, would have had an annual remittance?"

"That's correct."

"But when your father died, the solicitor drew the will from the safe, preparing to bring it to read out after the funeral and found that it named Anthony as heir and gave you a single bequest of five hundred pounds?" Pauline was beginning to think she was an actor in a stage farce.

"That's it."

"Then the solicitor called you and suggested holding off reading the will until an investigation could be made."

"Yes, and the police came, listened to what we had to say and took the will to check for fingerprints and for forged signatures," Frank Thornton said. "That's when the real nightmare began."

4

Pauline nodded, and said, "Because they've done that now and say it's in order. The signature is your father's and the will is genuine."

"Exactly. The will, they say, looks genuine enough and it stands," Thornton said.

"Aye," Alan said, breaking in on the tale, "but the difficulty is Tony Thornton wants to sell the land to the highest bidder, developers to be precise."

Pauline looked at Frank Thornton for confirmation.

He nodded. "My brother is a man who likes his life in London, Paris, St. Tropez and all those places the rich and idle go. Only, he can't really afford it on his present income. This lovely old estate and all the farms will be gone in a heartbeat, if this will stands, for he'll sell to the highest bidder."

"You're quite sure your father didn't change the will?" she asked, looking him squarely in the eye.

"I'm sure he did not," Thornton replied, "and so is our solicitor. He's as distraught over this as we all are. Somehow the will was changed and we have to prove it."

"You and your solicitor do realize, I suppose, that the only people who could have altered the will must work in the solicitor's office?"

Thornton hesitated before saying, "Naturally, we thought of that, but it isn't possible. John Ogilvie, his father, and his grandfather have been the Thornton family solicitors for almost a century. They hold that position of trust because they are eminently trustworthy. It is impossible to imagine anyone in their office doing such a thing."

"How else could it be done, then?" Pauline said, now fully incredulous of the blind, willful obstinacy of such a statement.

"Alan says you have found many amazing solutions to problems before. Indeed, even I have heard of your successes.

We hope you will be able to show how this was done and exonerate the Ogilvies of any wrongdoing."

"This is a matter for the police," Pauline said.

"The police have already stated that the will is genuine and there's no case to be investigated. Indeed, they practically accused me of trying to overturn it because I was upset at being cut out."

"If the will is genuine, as their experts proved, then that is the only conclusion to be drawn," Pauline said. She held up her hand to prevent the angry outburst she could see about to begin, and continued, "If the will is false, as you and the lawyer say, then it can only have been falsified in the solicitor's office. Unless they can show it was elsewhere at some time and they failed to check it hadn't been tampered with while outside their care, which isn't much of an improvement in their culpability, frankly."

"I don't like the tone of this," Thornton said. "Alan said you could help us but all I'm hearing is slanderous remarks about an honest man and his family's firm."

Pauline shook her head. "Then get a private investigator who will pander to your sensitivities. The answer to this will be bad for someone and pretending that it isn't one of the Thornton or Ogilvie families won't help you."

Frank Thornton's expression was thunderous but, with a visible effort, he said, "I thought you were a private investigator."

"I investigate puzzles privately and people do pay me for assisting them but I'm not in the business of being a private investigator. I take cases where people want the truth and, where appropriate, justice. Neither of these things appear to be wanted here."

"That's not true. Everyone here knows my father's wishes and this will doesn't reflect those wishes. He would never have left the estate to Tony who is a scoundrel and a leech.

Our father knew exactly what would happen to the estate he loved if it should ever fall into Tony's hands."

That gave Pauline a thought. "Could this be simply a prank by your brother? Knowing how you and your father thought of him, could he have substituted the will just to make mischief?"

"This is no prank, Miss Riddell," Thornton said. "My brother outruns his allowance every month and is constantly asking me for more money. He's sold almost everything that had been handed down to him that he could sell. This is the act of a desperate man who intends to ruin dozens of lives in order to keep enjoying a life far beyond his means."

"What did he have handed down to him?"

"He had the bulk of our mother's funds," Thornton said. "It was understood that I, as the first born, would have the estate and so he got the bulk of mother's money. He has spent it all, thousands of pounds wasted on drink, drugs and, well, let's say parties."

"What Mr. Thornton says is true, Pauline," Alan said. "Everyone hereabouts will vouch for that. Last time he came up here, two years ago now, the goings on at the Dower house scandalized the whole neighborhood. He still has the old Dower house, you see."

"Mr. Thornton, I understand your feelings and," Pauline said, "those of your tenants and the village at large but, I repeat, if you want to know the truth of this, you must allow an investigator to expose whoever has done this, even if it is someone inside your household or the Ogilvie law office. There can be no other way."

"I refuse to believe it is anyone we know or have known these past years," Thornton said.

"Then you should have no reason to refuse to have a proper investigation. Indeed, when you've thought about it further, you'll see that by not investigating properly you leave suspicion hanging over your household and the Ogilvie office. Would Mr. Ogilvie be against a thorough investigation?"

"I don't know."

"Shouldn't we ask him?"

Thornton frowned as he struggled with the idea of calling the family's loyal solicitors and suggesting such a thing while desperate for an answer that made sense before the estate and its people were destroyed.

"I will phone John and do my best to suggest it without destroying their confidence in me," he said at last.

"Their confidence in you? They work for you," Pauline said. Her years of dealing with boardroom quarrels, and the board's conflicts with suppliers, was outraged by the antiquated notions his speech suggested.

"Miss Riddell," Thornton said, "in the world where you work, that may be considered a sharp thing to say but here in the real world we value mutual relationships. It's true we pay them for specific services but in return they provide wide loyalty and support when we need it."

Pauline shrugged. "Do, or say, what you need to make it happen. If Mr. Ogilvie can't accept a fair investigation into how the will was switched, you may as well start packing now."

Thornton nodded and left the room abruptly.

Pauline looked at Alan questioningly.

"He'll call from the estate office," Alan said. "He won't be a moment."

"I hope not. I want to get back to mother. She needs me more than any of you do."

"Mother has a bad cold, Pauline. I and all the others here will lose our livelihoods and Mr. Thornton his whole estate."

"Mother has flu," Pauline said, "and people her age die from flu. You folks can find other investigators, but you want me to do it for free and in my two weeks annual holiday instead of looking after Mum and Dad."

Fortunately, before the argument grew worse, Frank Thornton returned. His expression was lighter than when he'd left.

"John Ogilvie would be happy to speak to you," he said. "He's frantic to find the original will and recover the damage his office appears to have done. He'll be at his office for the rest of the day if you will drop by."

## 2

# A HOPELESS TASK

LOOKING out from Alan's Land Rover on the way into the village, Pauline watched the snow, still thin but falling steadily, piling up at the roadside and in the fields, where the wind was shaping it into drifts. *We should be going back to our parents' farm at Troutsdale,* she thought, *not further away from it.*

"John Ogilvie is a good man," Alan said suddenly, breaking into her thoughts.

"I've no doubt," Pauline said, "but if that will is a forgery then it happened in his office and you got me involved with it under false pretences."

"I did not," Alan exclaimed, "the will is linked to the incidents."

"Poppycock," Pauline snapped. "You knew I'd give in on the incidents because they were harming ordinary people but you thought I'd never waste time on the landed gentry."

"I thought nothing of the sort," Alan replied, equally angry. "Don't you see? This is just the latest in these incidents and as nasty as the others."

"There's nothing 'latest' about this at all. The forgery

happened years ago and came to light now, coincidentally around the time of these admittedly unpleasant crimes."

"You don't know that. You only believe it," Alan said, "and in case you hadn't taken it properly into your elevated thinking, the will harms dozens of ordinary people and only one 'landed gentry', using your ugly term."

"Aren't the Thorntons landed gentry then?"

"Frank Thornton and his father before him are decent, hard-working people, not idle loafers, which is what that term implies. But, even if they weren't, the people who will be really hurt here are me, Bessie and our children and the two other tenant farmers of the Thornton estate. And they have families too."

Pauline nodded and sighed. "You're right, of course, it is always ordinary people who suffer in upheavals but I still say you've tricked me into investigating this will."

They drove on in silence until the lights of Goathland, lit early in the gathering gloom and flickering in the falling snow, announced their arrival.

John Ogilvie was much younger than Pauline had expected. Around thirty-five and clearly worried. His expression was grief-stricken. Alan introduced them and they sat in the office waiting area to talk.

"When Frank said he'd asked you to look into this, I had no idea who you were, Miss Riddell. My office deals only with civil matters so criminal investigations aren't part of our world. I'm told you have solved many difficult cases; I hope you can help us too. What can I tell you," Ogilvie said, "that will help you understand the situation?"

"Start by telling me about when the will was made and how it has been kept."

"The will is little more than an update to the will that Frank's dad inherited from. In fact, apart from the names and some changes to incorporate new legal terms, the will hasn't changed since the eighteenth century. The eldest son gets the estate and siblings get allowances. In the present family, there is only one surviving sibling and that's Anthony."

"So, the will was changed recently?" Pauline asked.

"Oh no, not recently. Shortly after the death of the original heir, Peter. He was killed in the war, so the changes happened in 1945."

"You weren't working here then," Pauline said.

Ogilvie shook his head. "I was still at school. My father and his clerk, Harry Teesdale, made the changes and the will was signed and locked in our archives, where it has been until I got it out about a week ago when I heard old Mr. Thornton was not going to survive very much longer. That's when I found it didn't say what it should say."

"What does Harry Teesdale say about the will? Surely he remembers what was written?"

"Unfortunately, Harry is dead. When my father retired from the business, old Harry retired too. That was about five years ago. He went off to live in Spain where I'm afraid he died only a year later."

"Did he have relatives in Spain?"

"No, nothing like that. He was a bachelor who rarely traveled so I suppose he saved much of his salary. Anyway, he purchased a house there later in life and spent his summer holidays in it for a number of years. When he retired, he sold his home here and moved to Spain, which he said was better for his rheumatism."

Pauline nodded but didn't point out what Ogilvie, as a lawyer, must know. Spain had no extradition treaty with the United Kingdom. If 'old Harry' switched the will, he couldn't have been brought to trial for it. This was more like a how-to-prove-the-will-a-forgery case, than a 'who dun it'.

"Was his death unexpected?" she asked.

"Well, it was an accident, so it was in a way. Harry was

past retirement age, of course, so practically three-score-years-and-ten, but he was as fit as a fiddle. He's believed to have drowned in a swimming accident in the Mediterranean. They never found his body."

"You know the police think the will is genuine," Pauline said.

"Of course. Frank and I called them in the moment I contacted him. We thought it would be easy for them to show it a forgery."

"What convinced them it wasn't?"

"Everything. The paper, the ink, and the signatures, everything is of the same vintage and all are genuine."

"May I see it?"

"Certainly," Ogilvie said. "Frank said you'd want to see it and I was to let you."

He was gone a moment, returning with the papers. Pauline took them and scanned through them. As he'd said, a very simple will. Only three pages, the bequests on the first page, the usual legalese on the second page, and the signatures on the third. Pauline shook her head in dismay. All a forger needed to do was use headed paper from the company, the company typewriter to type out the altered bequests on a new first page and the job was done. It was childishly simple. Only an employee in the office could have access to all those things and access to the archives to remove and replace. Old Harry may have been as honest as the day is long but somehow, he was persuaded into this one simple criminal act. Bribery? Blackmail? Or what? The who was easier to guess.

"No one looked at the will in the intervening years?" Pauline asked.

"No. Why would we?"

"I just want to be sure of the facts. Who took Harry's job as clerk?"

"We've had two. Neil, who wasn't satisfactory and was only with us a year, and the present clerk, Edward."

"Why wasn't Neil satisfactory?"

"He was unreliable, often late for work, often leaving early, sloppy in his bookkeeping, there were so many faults we couldn't risk keeping him."

"Did you do any checks to see if anything was missing when he left or things that had been tampered with?"

"You think the will was tampered with during Neil's time? I doubt he'd know what to do. And what would he stand to gain?"

Pauline almost stamped her foot at such obtuseness.

"If Anthony Thornton is the kind of man you all say he is, he could have paid Neil to find the will, re-type the first page and return it to the archives and all for a moderate sum of money," Pauline said.

"It's possible but the police say the paper and the ink are the same age on all pages."

"In a company as old as this one, I've no doubt paper and ink are sitting on shelves and in drawers waiting to be found and used."

"But Neil wasn't that clever, Miss Riddell. In fact, he wasn't clever at all, which was another failing that became clear early on."

"Then it has to have been done by good old Harry, who fled the country the moment he retired."

"Pauline!" Alan cried. "Harry was as straight as they come. He worked here all his life, man and boy. He would never have betrayed them like that. He just wouldn't."

"I have to agree, Miss Riddell. I know this must look bad for Harry in your eyes, but we who knew him will never believe it."

"It's as well you all live and work among trustworthy people," Pauline said acidly, and added, before either of them could protest, "Thank you for your help, Mr. Ogilvie, but I don't think there's a lot of point my investigating this at all."

"Miss Riddell, you must," Ogilvie said. "We have no one else to turn to who would understand the village."

"He's right, Pauline," Alan said. "You lived here. You know the people here. An investigator from Leeds or some other city would never understand."

Against her better judgment, Pauline said, "Let me think about this. After I've nursed mother, if there's any time left, I'll reconsider."

They left Ogilvie's office and set out for home. The snow wasn't growing seriously deeper, which made Pauline feel better. The drive back to her parent's farm might not be as bad as she'd feared and her car's heater actually worked.

"You must help, Polly," Alan said again, as they made their way slowly along the street.

"I said, I'd think about it," Pauline said. "Now, when you first arrived this morning, you told me about a lot of unpleasant, malicious incidents. Since then, all we've done is talk about the Thornton will. Are these incidents real or did you make them up because you thought I wouldn't bother to come for a forged will?"

"You can be pretty rude sometimes, Pauline. I don't make things up. They are real and they are nasty."

"Then tell me about them. I see no hope of sorting out the will when the most obvious solution can't be considered and nor can I see why you think the will is linked to these incidents."

"Bloody rude, I should have said," he hesitated while the Land Rover drove through a ford that was running high with melting slush and snow. "We're not telling you not to consider Harry, just don't get fixated on him. He's the least likely person, even if he's the most obvious suspect."

"He's obvious for so many reasons. There's a good reason to think he had motive and he certainly had the opportunity."

"Just don't get blinkers on, is all we're saying."

"I don't wear blinkers," Pauline replied, adding silently *not any more anyway*, before saying, "now tell me about these incidents."

"They started small," Alan said. "We think shoplifting at the post office was the first but the last was housebreaking and they had quite a haul of silverware taken."

"How many?"

"Five so far and all over the neighborhood," Alan said.

"Someone with a car or similar vehicle then or they couldn't carry away a load of silver plate."

"Which is why we don't think children anymore, like we did at first."

"Could be someone taking advantage of children's mischief?" Pauline said thoughtfully.

"I suppose so," Alan said, "but even the first incidents had a nastiness about them that was more than naughtiness."

"In what way?"

"Old Miss Goforth had one of her cats hung up outside her door and Bill Watson, the retired policeman, had his retirement clock smashed to smithereens and his service medals stolen. These things were very specific, pointed directly to something the person was proud of or they loved absolutely."

"I agree. It doesn't sound like children, not young ones anyway. Why do you think they're linked to the will? The two crimes seem totally unrelated."

"Polly, how long have we lived in this neighborhood? Has there ever been anything like these two things in all that time? One, mebbe, though I can't think of one. Two, never? Somehow, they're linked and, of the two, I put the will as the more serious."

"It does seem odd, as you say, but coincidences happen, and times are changing. There are new people in the area and that alone means change," Pauline replied.

"Both of these crimes have local knowledge behind them. They aren't something new. They're something old. Now, you must come in and say goodnight to Bessie and the bairns," Alan said, suddenly turning off the road and down the rutted, broken track that led to his farm. "You hardly had time to say 'Merry Christmas' to the children when we set out and they'll want to see their auntie."

"Alan, we don't have time now. We told mum two hours. We've been away nearly four now. She'll be sure we're lying dead in a ditch."

"Just pop in and say hello and we'll be gone," Alan said, totally unmoved by thoughts of his mother's concerns.

But it was her mother that Pauline was concerned about. Over the past week, from her home near Newcastle, she'd talked on the phone with her father and it was his obvious concern, though he was desperately trying to hide it, that had made up Pauline's mind. Her mother had come down with flu, not an unusual occurrence for wintertime in the north of England where the cold and damp gave everyone colds each year, but her father said this was worse than anything he'd seen.

After speaking with her father, Pauline had called the local village doctor, Forsythe, and his tone was equally somber. Her mother was not fighting this off as once she might have.

"She's only in her fifties," Pauline had said, dismayed by this defeatism.

"She won't have told you this, Miss Riddell, but she's grown quite frail this past year."

"Then why didn't you do anything about it?"

"Because I didn't know," he replied. "You know how

folks around here are. They don't go to doctors until they're actually at death's door. It wasn't until I visited her on Tuesday I saw how thin she'd grown."

That Pauline could believe, and she said so. "Did you ask about her weight-loss?"

"She said she's been dieting and was pleased to get back to her girlish figure."

"I was thinking of coming down there and nursing her," Pauline said, "but I'm not sure I won't be driven to murder her."

Doctor Forsythe laughed. "She's your mother, Miss Riddell. You might be forgiven for doing that, I won't."

So, Pauline had booked time off work, taking the days she'd saved for the Christmas and New Year period in 1962 and adding one week of her 1963 vacation, to ensure her mother was properly nursed and even forced to take her medicine for once in her life.

"We'll talk about what we can do after you've spent time with the young 'uns," Alan said, breaking into her dark thoughts.

Pauline didn't answer. Here she was, being pressed by her brother into investigating minor village wrongdoings when her mother's life was at stake. Well, she wouldn't do it and Alan could put that in his pipe and smoke it. But she'd find a more diplomatic way to tell him when she'd thought about it some more.

## 3

# ANOTHER HOPELESS TASK

AN HOUR LATER, however, as Pauline fumed in silent indignation, they were still at Alan's farm and no opportunity to disabuse Alan had presented itself because Alan disappeared the moment they'd arrived. He'd said he had a few odd jobs to do. He'd be back in a jiffy and they'd talk about what to do next. Pauline ground her teeth and made small talk with Bessie, who was busy preparing the evening meal and clearly wishing Pauline gone as much as Pauline wished to be gone.

"Are there new people in the village?" Pauline asked.

"New people in the village?" Bessie said. "No, not recently. There's nothing for a new person to do here and we don't have any spare houses for retirees to move into."

Pauline frowned. "No rental houses at all?"

"Not really," Bessie said, "other than Anthony Thornton's mother's old house. You'll remember it – The Dower house. He rents it out in summer when he can, but then he always has rented it. It hardly ever gets guests, there's nothing to do around here except hike on the moors and that isn't much of a holiday for most folks nowadays. Though he did let it this past autumn."

"Is there someone there now?"

"I shouldn't think so. There was a Frenchwoman there in the fall. She was an artist, supposed to be painting local scenes. I don't know if she's still there. I doubt it. I wouldn't be if I had somewhere warmer to be. This is a cold winter, and nothing's been done to that old house in living memory except occasional repairs."

"Did the woman join in any of the village events?"

"Nay, why would she? She were only here to paint pictures."

"I just wondered what she was like."

"Mrs. Drayton, who keeps the post office, is the only one who really saw her. She said she wore too much makeup, but Mrs. Drayton is a Methodist and doesn't hold with such things."

"Not much of a description," Pauline said, smiling.

"She said the woman was slim and well enough looking, for a foreigner."

Pauline laughed. "Mrs. Drayton has an acute eye for detail, I can tell."

"I don't know about that," Bessie said, "unless it's something out of the ordinary in the mail. She sniffs that out all right."

With that, Pauline had to be content. And, in the end, why was she asking? If the woman was gone, she couldn't be responsible for the later incidents, which were the ones that were most disturbing. What she needed to know was when the woman left. That way she could be sure it really was nothing to do with her. But it was suspicious, a foreigner coming all this way to paint. Why here? The landscape was certainly wild and rugged but hardly the subject for artists; there wasn't enough variety to the land for a picture. Miles of heather but no foreground, middle ground or background. Just a sea of heather that stretched to the horizon, a beautiful

20

purple quilt in late summer but dull gray-green the rest of the year, under an invariably lowering, cloudy sky. Still, even though she was not going to investigate, Pauline thought she should see if Mrs. Drayton knew more than she'd told Bessie.

Finally, with the light going, Alan could find no more jobs to do and returned to the house, where he immediately pronounced it too late for more talk and warned Pauline she'd need to be really careful driving back to Troutsdale in the dark. Too angry to take a civil leave of him, Pauline stormed out of the house and into her now snow-covered car. Clearing the snow off it with her expensive kidskin gloves didn't improve her temper.

Arriving back at her parent's farm in a heavy snow shower, she parked as close to the kitchen door as she could. She leapt from the car, ran to the door, opened it and stepped inside to see her mother, wrapped in blankets and an ancient dressing gown, heating soup over their old Aga stove.

"Mum! What are you doing?"

"Your dad and I needed something hot and you were off gallivanting, so I came to make it myself. You said you'd be back hours ago."

"You've your precious Alan to thank for my not being here. He dragged me across half the dale and then took me to his place to talk with Bessie, who's been wishing me gone this past hour. Take your complaint up with him when next you see him."

"Oh, if Alan wanted you to meet people, there'll be a good reason."

Pauline took the stirring spoon from her mother's hand and struggled not to smack the woman with it. Instead, she said, "You! Back to bed. I'll bring up the soup as soon as it's hot."

"Your dad wanted a hot toddy of honey and whisky too."

"Go!" Pauline said thunderously, pointing to the door to

the stairs. Her mother left and Pauline turned back to the stove. The kettle sounded like it would soon boil so she retrieved a glass from the cupboard, the whisky from her father's drink cabinet, and honey from the pantry. When the hot toddy was ready, she marched it upstairs to her father who was sitting up in bed, wearing his dressing gown, with the blankets pulled up to his chin.

Pauline placed the glass on his bedside table and glared at him.

"Don't look at me like that," her father said. "You know what your mother is like. If she's going to do something, she does it. No one can stop her."

"You're her husband, Dad. You're supposed to have some influence."

"You two do know I'm right here," her mother said from the other side of the bed.

"We know, Mum, and we're both angry with you."

"I'm not an invalid and you weren't here."

"Dad could have got what you wanted."

"I didn't want anything," Mrs. Riddell snapped. "But your dad is coming down with my cold and I wanted him to have something hot. We can't both of us be sick."

Mr. Riddell struggled to keep a straight face as he watched Pauline's expression pass from angry, through livid, to incandescent rage.

Unable to stop herself, Pauline cried, "Mother, you're sick. You don't have a cold, you have flu. The doctor said so and you have to stay in bed until a doctor says you can leave it."

"What do doctors know," her mum snorted in disdain. "Do they have a house to run? Chickens to manage? Beasts to feed?"

"Mother," Pauline said in a voice that would have frightened Attila the Hun if he'd heard it. "You stay where you are.

Don't move, don't even think about moving. I'll bring you both hot soup in ten minutes. And Dad, stop grinning like an idiot!"

She stormed out of the bedroom and pounded down the stairs. Her mother was impossible. She loved her dearly, of course, but how poor Dad had put up with her all these years, Pauline was often at a loss to explain.

By the time the soup was hot, ladled into bowls, and on a tray, Pauline was a little calmer. She took deep breaths as she climbed the stairs, determined to be all sweetness and light when she entered the room.

Upon entering the room, however, she found the bedroom window had been opened and a small gale was blowing snowflakes into the room.

"What are you doing?" Pauline demanded.

"It was stuffy in here," her mother said, "We needed air."

"The doctor said to keep warm not freeze the germs or yourself to death," Pauline cried, placing the bowls on their side tables before crossing the room to close the window. Outside, the snow swirled in the faint light from the room's window and its two small bedside lamps. There were no other lights along the whole valley. Even those farms that now had electricity were still not going to waste it. Yorkshire folk were famous for their careful ways.

"I'm going to light a fire in here," Pauline said, "then you can take those gowns and extra blankets off. It will help you sleep better."

"Waste of coal," her mother and father said, almost in unison.

"You are not going to make yourself even more ill to save a few pennies," Pauline said. "I'll buy the coal myself if that will make you feel better about it."

"Nay, lass," her father said. "You mebbe right. A bit of

luxury for the sick at Christmas can be excused. Though I don't hold with all that other malarkey."

"If by *malarky* you mean gifts, feasting, and general merriment," Pauline said, "you're out of luck. I've invited all the family over on Boxing Day and I want you two on your feet and well, which is why mother is staying in bed and doing everything the doctor said to do until then."

"We've been too busy for shopping," her mother protested.

"I will do that tomorrow and Alan will be here to manage the animals so you both can forget you're Yorkshire folk and enjoy yourself for once."

Finding that they had no further arguments to make, Pauline went downstairs to find paper, kindling and coal. Armed with her fire-lighting supplies, she returned to their room and lit the fire. The chimney smoked badly at first and she was forced to re-open the window, which at least made her mother laugh. Eventually, the chimney warmed, the smoke rose, and the fire was glowing brightly in the grate.

"Now it doesn't feel quite so much like we're living in Scrooge's house," Pauline said, satisfied at the result. "I'll get more coal and the cards. We'll play until you're tired."

## FREED TO INVESTIGATE – DECEMBER 22

BY NEXT MORNING, when the fires had gone out in the house, the old stone building felt exactly like Scrooge's home. With shivering hands, Pauline re-lit the fire in the living room, put more wood in the Aga, and prepared hot porridge for her parents' breakfast.

"I like bacon and eggs," her father said when she took breakfast up to them. They were both once again wrapped in gowns and extra blankets.

"Then you should make some when you're up," Pauline snapped.

"Nay, lass," her mother said sharply. "I'll not have him messing about in my kitchen. If you can't make them, I will." She tried to throw off the covers, but Pauline got there first and sat on them.

"You, Mother, aren't going anywhere until the doctor says so," she said. "I thought I'd made that clear."

"You're not master nor mistress of this house," her mother said, bristling.

"Until the doctor releases you, I am mistress here, Mother, and you'd better do everything in your power to get well or you'll never be rid of me."

"I'm perfectly well," her mother protested. "The fever's gone, the chills are gone. I'm as right as rain."

"Dr. Forsythe will be here at eleven," Pauline said, handing her mother the bowl of porridge, "and if he says you can get up. Then you can."

"Hah!" her mother said triumphantly. "Then you'll have to collect the eggs if I can't get up."

"I'll do that after I have the fire lit in this room and had my breakfast," Pauline said. "I don't trust you not to wriggle out of bed the moment my back is turned."

They ate their breakfasts together in the cold, dark room where frost had made intricate patterns on the window. Pauline knew from experience the ice's intricate tracery was inside the glass and not outside. She said nothing but fervently wished she was back in her own centrally heated home.

She picked up the tray of dishes and said, "I'll be back with tea and kindling to light this fire."

"Aye," her father said, "that'll give me time to get dressed. I've work to do, tha knows."

"You can get up, Dad," Pauline said, staring down her mother's furious gaze, "but you, Mother, can't!"

It was nine o'clock by the time she was ready to collect the eggs from the henhouse, the only new building on the farm. Its narrow windows, set high up but below the overhanging corrugated roof, glowed from the lights inside. The light illuminated icicles hanging from the roof that sloped down almost to the ground. They were taller than Pauline. She grinned, remembering having sword fights with her brothers, using icicles from the farm buildings when she was a child. These icicles were so big, they'd have been lances for them, not swords.

Inside the building, the heat from hundreds of hens, and the heating from the lamps, was a pleasant change from the outside air and even the house. It was typical of her parents, and maybe all farmers, that the animals were housed warmer than people were. She gathered the eggs from their straw-lined shelves, brushing aside indignant hens, until her basket was full and becoming too heavy to carry safely. However, she managed not to slip and fall, which would have broken the best part of a week's earnings for the farm, as she made her way slowly back to the house.

She was still washing, drying, and placing the eggs in the cartons that they were to be transported in, when the doctor arrived.

"Dr. Forsythe," Pauline said, as he stepped inside. "I hope you'll see enough improvement in Mother to let her loose. I really can't be responsible for her actions, or my own, if you don't."

He laughed. "She's a poor patient," he agreed, "but they all are around here."

"You should buy a practice in Leeds or some other city where rich people pretend to be ill, you pretend to cure them, and all at real private consulting fees."

"Then I'd never get paid in pheasants and partridge," Forsythe said. "There are benefits to dealing with farmers, you know."

"You must like pheasant a lot, Doctor," Pauline said. "Anyway, go up and for goodness sake, let her loose."

Fortunately for Pauline, the doctor did agree Mrs. Riddell was now well enough to get out of bed as long as she kept warm and rested – no heavy farm work!

"Mum can bunk in with the hens," Pauline said, when she ushered the doctor out. "It's warmer in their house than it is in this one."

With her mother up, and she was up and dressed before the doctor's car had left the farmyard, Pauline found she was going to have time on her hands during the rest of her stay.

She was firmly told by her mother that she didn't need any help, thank you, and Pauline, as a guest, should sit down and enjoy her visit. Pauline decided instead to visit Mrs. Drayton, the postmistress at Goathland, tomorrow morning, and in the meantime supervise her mother as best as anyone could.

# 5

# THE FRENCH PAINTER – DECEMBER 23

NEXT DAY, from the Goathland Post Office window, Pauline watched the children as they industriously built their snow fort from the compressed blocks of snow left behind by the bulldozer as it cleared the road down the valley side, through the village, and up the opposite side of the valley. She smiled, remembering her own childhood and the igloos she and her brothers and sisters had built in the snow-covered garden at the farm.

From where she stood, the children looked like a line of ants stretched out from the fort to the road, each carrying one or, in the case of the bigger kids, two blocks. The blocks were cut out by the vehicle's caterpillar tracks and left behind as it moved forward over the snow. The children, bundled in woolen coats, mitts, hats, and scarves, labored patiently. What had clearly begun as a snow wall had now been given a square tower, or turret, with new walls appearing as its outer defenses. She wondered, for a moment, if this was a race memory of the violent times in the North only a few hundred years ago or whether it was a human instinct; one that a fleshy creature with inadequate teeth and claws but an outsize brain might always replicate wherever it went in a world of flesh-eating predators. Whatever the truth, the fort was quickly becoming large enough to rival some of the castles in the neighboring countryside for the children showed no signs of tiring of this game while the bulldozer was working.

It was the bulldozer that Pauline hoped wouldn't tire, for her only hope of getting out of the valley, the dale, and back to her own home and work lay along the road it was clearing. The radio spoke of helicopters dropping food to people and farm stock in other lonely areas of the country. None had mentioned this happening on the land to the north of Yorkshire so she felt confident that if she could get her car up the valley side, she could get back to her home. Meanwhile, she was freezing her extremities off in old-fashioned accommodation in the wilds of Yorkshire's North Riding with nothing but the radio and some books to make the dark winter afternoons and nights bearable. She couldn't imagine why she looked back on her childhood, which was actually worse than this for there wasn't even electricity then, with such fondness.

"Will that be everything, Miss Riddell?" the postmistress asked.

"Sorry, I was wool-gathering," Pauline said, opening her handbag to find her purse. "Watching the children reminded me of my own childhood and the time we spent building snow forts, though we didn't have such an efficient snow block builder as they have."

"They'll all have chilblains by tomorrow," Mrs. Drayton said. Her disapproving expression said she wouldn't be sorry if that were true.

"The Frenchwoman you told me about," Pauline said, hoping she was not being too obvious, "did she say why she came here? It seems a strange place to visit unless you have a connection here."

"She did, now you mention it. She said she'd met Mr. Anthony Thornton at the Riviera and he'd encouraged her to come and paint the moors. Even let her rent the house at a bargain price."

"Ah! I thought it must have been something like that," Pauline said.

"You don't suspect her of those horrible incidents, do you? She were gone before any of that nonsense started."

Pauline smiled and shook her head. "It was just my curiosity," she said. "We had painters stay on the farm after the war, and Gran said they did after the previous war too, but since then, none I think."

"Aye, that's true. It was good for the soldiers to come out into the peace of the country and recover. She weren't anything like that, though. She were a lively one."

"How? In what way, I mean?"

"Lots of spring in her step," Mrs. Drayton said. "Talked about the good walks she was enjoying, that sort of thing."

"What did she look like?"

"She'd have looked better with less makeup but there's no accounting for modern women or foreigners."

Mrs. Drayton was probably fifty but aspired to look more mature, Pauline thought with a secret smile.

"I imagine in the South of France, where I understand Anthony Thornton has his home, makeup is the usual uniform of women who wish to be fashionable," Pauline said.

"Aye, but so do our own young folk now. I don't hold with it and neither did Mr. Drayton. God rest his soul."

"I must get back," Pauline said, handing over the money for her few purchases. "The days draw in so quickly, don't they, and I've got lots of shopping to do."

"Aye, we lose the sun early being down here in the dale," Mrs. Drayton said, handing Pauline her change. "Careful walking back, it gets very slippery underfoot when the warmth is gone."

"Do you remember the woman's name?" Pauline said, pausing at the shop door.

Mrs. Drayton grimaced. "Nicole, I think. Something like that."

Pauline chose to return to Alan and Bessie's house, where she'd parked her car, by way of the old Dower house. It wasn't the most direct route, in fact it was a long way out of her way, but she needed to confirm the house was indeed empty. The house was set back from the road behind tall, iron gates and a long drive. She stopped and surveyed the house and grounds. Like the manor to which it had once belonged, it was old, probably Seventeenth Century and, like the manor, it also hadn't been modified since. Whether this was because the Thornton's had never been rich enough or whether they just didn't believe in making changes to something they'd thought perfect on the day they bought or built it, she couldn't know but so it was.

One good thing about the snow was she could see that Mrs. Drayton was probably right. The Frenchwoman was gone. There wasn't a human footprint on the snow anywhere at the front of the house. Nor were there any lights on in the house and most of the windows had shades drawn. No smoke curled up from the chimneys. The house looked as empty as the postmistress had said it was.

Pauline followed the road to the edge of the property. A narrow path ran down the side of the garden fence, heading toward the back of the house and gardens. It too had untouched snow. Even village people seemed to have no need to visit this lonely place on the edge of the village. Pauline wondered what dowagers down the years thought of it. Maybe they were happy to be so separate from the rest of the world but, on balance, she thought not. After a lifetime of being the leading woman in the neighborhood, it would seem like exile, punishment even, to many.

She looked at the sky, still heavy with clouds and pregnant with snow. She checked her watch. Less than an hour of daylight left, though, thanks to those low clouds that seemed to touch the valley rim at either side, dusk would come early again this afternoon. Still, she felt there was time to view the back of the house and be home before dark.

The rear of the house told a different story from the front. Clear footprints marked a trail from the back door of the house to the small gate in the low garden wall. Maybe this house had been burgled too? With no one in it for weeks, who would know? Did the estate steward come to check on the house? If so, were these his footprints and not those of a burglar? She thought she should tell the police but, before she did, she'd check with Frank Thornton.

When she phoned him from home, Frank Thornton confirmed what Pauline had guessed would be the case. Brother Anthony wouldn't let Frank's estate steward, or anyone else associated with the estate, enter the property. The honorable Anthony had said he would employ his own people to do that. Frank had no idea if he did and couldn't explain the footprints in the snow beyond guessing there was a regular visitor who made sure the house was in good order. Failing that, sadly, there probably had indeed been a house-breaking.

Her next phone call was to Constable Wilson, the Goath-land village 'bobby', who seemed more puzzled as to what Pauline was doing snooping around another person's property than taking note of a possible burglary.

"My brother told me of the string of malicious incidents in the weeks leading up to Christmas," Pauline said. "I learned there was a woman staying at the old Dower house at least part of the time, which you already knew, I'm sure. When I was also told the woman had gone, I wanted to be sure. I wanted to eliminate her from my enquiries, you might say."

"You didn't enter the property at all?" Wilson asked.

"I did not."

"Good. I don't want to go there, investigate everything and find it is you we're chasing."

Pauline laughed. "My footprints go to the outside gate and not inside," she said. "Anyway, it is snowing again so my prints might be hard to find. The trails inside the grounds, however, were well-marked and not likely to have been erased by one night's snow."

"We'll look into it, Miss Riddell," Constable Wilson said, sounding just like Dixon of *Dock Green* on the television. Pauline didn't have a television, but Dixon had leapt from the small screen into everyday life. He'd become a national icon that no one could be unaware of. He continued, "I hope you aren't involving yourself in Police business, Miss Riddell. It isn't safe for the public to become embroiled with criminals."

## 6

## CHRISTMAS EVE

NEXT DAY, Constable Wilson saw Pauline in the short main street of the village where she was buying the groceries the farm didn't produce for itself, and hailed her.

"I followed up the information you gave, Miss Riddell," he said. "There's a real estate agent from Whitby who has the keys to check the old house isn't flooded or anything like that. He's the one who's been going in and out."

Pauline was puzzled. "How often does he visit?" she asked. "The trails I saw were more than one visit."

"He goes in weekly," Wilson replied. "That's the insurance company's requirement."

"And he goes every week, once per week?"

"He does. Every Tuesday, immediately after lunch at the hotel, he inspects the property and makes a note of it for the insurance company records."

"Well, thank you for looking into it, Constable," she said. "I still think there were too many footprints for one visit by one man but possibly he went back out to his car for something and returned. Something like that would account for it, perhaps."

As Wilson rode away on his bike, Pauline decided that, as

it was now past the time when the agent was supposed to inspect the Dower house this week, the very next Tuesday she would watch the house and see what happened. Meanwhile, she had work to do, shopping and preparing for tomorrow's Christmas feast, though a small feast for just herself and her parents.

# 7

# A MURDER FOR CHRISTMAS – DECEMBER 25

CHRISTMAS DAY BEGAN EARLY for Pauline and her mother as they raked out ashes, kindled a fire in the living room, and relit the Aga stove. The goose had been cleaned the day before and was hanging in the pantry awaiting the sage and onion stuffing they were making, their most important job of the morning. Once the bird had been made ready and put in the oven to roast, Pauline quickly placed the presents she'd brought for her parents under the tree her father had brought inside some days earlier. Mentally, Pauline thanked her lucky stars her mother's illness had caused the rest of the family to organize their Christmases in their own homes otherwise this morning would have been doubly stressful.

When the doctor had declared Mrs. Riddell flu-free, her parents had been invited to Christmas dinner at all her local brothers' and sisters' homes, but, being themselves, they'd refused to go to any.

"Christmas away from home," her mother said, when Pauline pressed her to accept one of the invitations, "whatever next? And who would we pick without offending the others? And don't tell me we could go to the others in future years. Your dad and I aren't so old yet that we can't manage our own lives."

So Pauline spent the morning scraping potatoes and carrots, steaming the Christmas pudding, which was making the windows run with condensation, preparing the parsnips and Brussels sprouts, setting the table, and all the other jobs a traditional Christmas dinner meant, while her mother fussed and scurried from pan to pan ensuring everything was the way she wanted.

After breakfast they exchanged gifts and, always the best part for Pauline, inspected the contents of her Christmas stocking. She was pleased with everything she found; a clementine, Brazil nuts, walnuts, hazelnuts, Fry's mint chocolate bar, Thornton's toffees, and Turkish Delight. Even the fact she'd bought and put almost everything in there didn't dim her pleasure.

By lunchtime, regaled with cherry brandy and Advocaat, that newly fashionable Dutch mixture of egg yolks and alcohol, the two women were once again on good terms with each other.

"Do you remember that nice teashop in Scarborough?" her mother asked, as they sat comfortably around the blazing fire waiting for the Queen's Speech at three pm.

"I do. Is it still there?"

"Yes and no. The woman who used to own it has retired and the new people, though they're very good, well, it's not the same," her mother said wistfully.

"I'm sorry to hear that," Pauline said. "I liked our treats there."

"I did too," she gave Pauline a beaming smile and a sudden bone-crushing hug. "I miss having my girls at home."

Pauline was tempted to retort that her mother could be a little less sharp when she had one at home but in the interests of harmony and the season, she simply smiled and hugged her back. In truth, she was worried. She thought her parents looked older and not so well, her mother particularly seemed frail at times. She would have assumed her mother was just growing naturally older, but Dr. Forsythe's earlier words now made her anxious.

They had a late Christmas dinner, everything being ready by about four o'clock and had just retired to the cozy sitting room, with yet another cherry brandy enjoying the blazing fire her father had stirred up with the poker, when they heard the outer door open, followed by a cold draft from the outside world.

Her father got up to investigate but before he'd even left the room, Alan stepped into it.

"Polly, you're needed," he said. "I knew it would come to this."

"What are you talking about?" Pauline said, too warm and full to be interested in loud brothers and cryptic statements.

Alan, tripping over his words in his excitement, told her their cousin Walter, a constant playmate when they were children, had been found dead that morning in a snow-filled hollow by a neighbor. He ended this by saying, "Now will you help?"

At first, Pauline could hardly understand what he was saying it was so mangled, but when she did, it made her blood run cold. Her mind went back many years to a snowy day when she was about thirteen. She and Walter were hiding, a pile of snowballs made ready beside them, waiting to ambush her approaching, unsuspecting brothers and sisters. She turned to Walter, smiling and excited. He kissed her. Just lightly on her lips. Her expression must have told Walter all he needed to know for he drew her close and kissed her again and no longer lightly.

Pauline shook her head to banish the thoughts and return to the present. She'd hoped to minimize her involvement with the forged will and the criminal incidents that had plagued the village and surrounding farms in the weeks before Christmas, but now this, a crime her conscience said she had to solve.

"What would Walter have been doing out overnight in this weather?" she asked, trying to put off giving him a reply. Her immediate concern must still be for her mother. "It may have been an accident."

"It was no accident," Alan replied. "His head was hit hard, more than once."

"He could have fallen and hit his head."

"Not Walter. He's out nearly every night in all weathers, has been for years and he's as sure footed as a cat. He knows the moors better than anyone living."

"Why is he out every night?"

Alan looked embarrassed. "He does a bit of poaching, and well, this and that," he said.

"Poaching! In this weather?"

"There's always something to catch whatever the weather," Alan said, "and he had other side businesses that are best done in darkness."

Pauline was horrified. Walter was family and someone she'd known, played with when a child and shared her first teenage kiss with. How did he get into crime? She knew country folk didn't see poaching as a crime. But, 'Other business best done in darkness'? She took that to mean some smuggling of contraband foreign goods from the trawlers that worked out of, or put into, Whitby and Scarborough.

"He was a criminal, in fact," she said.

"That's a bit hard," her father said, suddenly interjecting. "He helped people with things they needed but couldn't easily get on their income."

"Ha!" Pauline retorted. "The wine and brandy won't have been for poor people, you can be sure."

"We all have desires that are above our income, Pauline,

and there's no harm in it. No one is hurt except the government has to be a bit careful with its money like, as they don't get their share of this."

"My taxes, all our taxes, are higher because they don't get this revenue."

"Nay," Alan said, determined to take back control of the discussion. "You know full well they tax what they want; this bit of revenue makes no difference at all. If they got those taxes, they'd spend it on yet more rubbish. Anything held back from those people is a benefit to all of us. Anyway, poaching and a bit of side business aren't a capital offence yet. You have to help now."

Pauline had expected this argument and she knew she had little choice. Walter may have become the black sheep but he was still family. If he was murdered and it wasn't an accident, she had to do something. Everyone would expect it. Besides, she wondered guiltily, would Walter have become what he did if he'd had a steadier head to guide him?

"Very well. Let me get dressed in some warmer clothes."

Her parents too looked ready to start dressing.

"Where do you think you're going?" Pauline said to her mother. "You stay here and keep warm and you, Dad, stay here to make sure Mum does stay."

"Walter was family," her mother said. "Alive, he was a criminal and we kept our distance, it's true, but dead he's family."

"The body will have been moved by the Police, Mum," Pauline said, as patiently as she could. "You'll just make yourself ill by coming. Stay here and think about organizing his funeral. That's the best thing you can do for him right now."

"Pauline's right, love," her father said. "We'll stay and sort out what's to be done."

Her mother paused, but then, after some very minor quibbling, which confirmed she wasn't really seriously considering going out, she agreed to stay, and Pauline ran upstairs to change.

WHEN ALAN WAS PULLING out of the yard and onto the track up to the road, Pauline said, "They'll start misbehaving when they're sure I'm gone, you know. Really, they're worse than children."

"It's second childhood with them," Alan agreed.

"That's why I have to keep them guessing. I said we're going to be back in an hour, that way they can't get up to too much mischief."

Alan laughed. "They'll know it'll be longer and be partying when we return."

As they both knew her parents weren't the party type, this idea, and the additional ideas it suggested, amused them until they arrived at Walter's cottage and parked outside.

"His body was found out on the moors. It's not far," Alan said, when he saw Pauline staring out across the snow-covered moorland.

"How far?" she demanded. "And isn't there a road where we can park nearer?"

"Nay," Alan said, shaking his head. "What have they done to you in yon great city? You were always first out into the snow once."

Sighing, Pauline pulled her collar up, buttoned to the chin, and set out following her brother. All these, 'you weres' were just another way of them getting their way, she could see that. Unfortunately, it was too effective.

The body was gone from the hollow by the time Pauline had arrived at the scene. All that remained was the shape in the snow where it had been and trampled snow around the shape where searchers, police, and ambulance crews had muddied the clean white drifts burying the heather.

She looked around. The golf balls loomed high on the ridge above the moors to her right and the moors rolled away, snow white, to the horizon in every other direction. A lonely spot to die. But if he was murdered, two people were out here in the middle of a winter night during one of the coldest, snowiest nights of the coldest and snowiest winters in modern times. Why?

"Are there any homes near here?" Pauline asked.

"Aye," Alan replied. "There's Walter's where we just came from, you can't see it now because it's in a hollow, and then the village too is only a mile over the other way. Brand's farm is over that way," he added, pointing to the horizon between the directions he'd given her. "Don't you remember aught of your life here?"

"I don't recognize it in all this winter wonderland of snow," Pauline said. "Honestly, I don't remember ever seeing it like this."

Alan nodded. "I suppose that's true. We didn't visit here much in winter when we were bairns. We stayed on the farm."

"Why was he here and why was someone else here?" Pauline said.

"Presumably because he was meeting the person and they fell out," Alan replied.

"If you want to meet someone on a dark winter's night in the worst weather we've seen in years, you go where there's shelter. This is madness."

Alan nodded. "I see what you mean," he said.

"We need to speak to the police and forensics," Pauline said. "Maybe he was killed elsewhere and his body dumped here."

"Will they tell us?"

"Maybe not but we're relatives so we can ask. Let's go. I'm freezing."

Alan laughed. "You've spent too much time indoors in your new life," he said. "You've gone soft."

Soft is exactly how Pauline was feeling but soft in the heart and head. *Oh, Walter*, she thought, as Alan drove them away from the cottage, *why couldn't you change*? He'd been so easy to love but too wild for her, even then.

CONSTABLE WILSON at the village police station wasn't impressed by their requests to meet the officer in charge and it took some time before they were able to persuade him. When they did, however, they found the detective inspector, who'd traveled in from Whitby, to be more helpful.

"The victim was your cousin?" DI Peacock asked.

"Yes," Pauline said, "and one we've known all our lives."

"His being suspected, and found guilty of, poaching and also suspected of smuggling wasn't a bar to your relationship?"

"I wasn't aware of it," Pauline said indignantly. "I've lived away from here for more than ten years now."

"No one mentioned it to you?"

"That's because she's become famous for helping the police do their job," Alan said. "You lot can't do without her up there in Newcastle, apparently."

"I thought the name was familiar," Peacock said, with a grin. "May I give you some advice, Miss Riddell?"

"You may. I don't promise to follow it."

"My advice is you don't approach the senior officers back at HQ for anything. They have strong views about interference from the public and even stronger views about private detectives."

"And you, DI Peacock?"

"I believe in taking help from wherever I can get it, Miss Riddell."

"Then will you tell me something about my cousin's body and where he was found? With that, I may be able to help."

"We await the pathologist's report on the body, Miss Riddell," Peacock said. "I may be able to answer those questions tomorrow or the day after. As to where he was found, there's not a lot to say."

"Can you say if he was killed there or not?"

"Ah, yes, good question. We think not."

"Any particular reason?"

"Not enough blood for one thing. Head wounds bleed like anything, as I'm sure you know. Also, it was hard to tell, but there seems to be only one set of footprints out to where his body was found. We think he was killed at home and someone carried and dragged the body out before dumping it, hoping the snow would hide it for some time."

"How was he found?"

"The killer's bad luck. Your cousin had agreed to meet with a friend last night and the friend called at the house. He found the lights on and a fire lit but no one home. On investigating, he saw the trail of prints leading out from the back door. Concerned your cousin may have had an accident, he followed them to the body."

"Were you able to get anything from the footprints?"

"Unfortunately, your cousin's friend didn't know they were the killer's footprints and walked on them himself. We have some small pieces of print but nothing that will likely prove useful."

"I see. Disappointing," Pauline said. "During your investigation, if you learn anything relating to the unpleasant incidents that have plagued the village these past weeks, which Constable Wilson is looking into, you will let me know, won't you?"

"Have they anything to do with the murder, Miss Riddell?"

"I don't know, but I was asked to look into an apparently forged will of the Thornton family and told about the incidents, with the suggestion they are linked, and now this happens. Perhaps, they're not linked to the will but if this is a robbery gone wrong then the incidents and the murder may well be the work of the same culprit."

Peacock nodded. "Could be," he said. "Any possible leads are good right now, so we'll do that."

"I will keep you informed of my progress, Inspector. I hope you will return the favor."

"That's not how these things are supposed to work."

"It's how they will work if you hope to hear anything more from me," Pauline said sharply.

Peacock laughed. "I'm sure there will be lots to discuss, Miss Riddell, and ideas exchanged. But I can't divulge police business, you know."

"Quite right. That would be very wrong. Well, as I look into the legitimacy of the will, I'm going to follow up on those puzzling incidents, which may have nothing to do with the murder, so I won't be disturbing your investigation at all."

"I'm sure Constable Wilson is investigating the incidents so you'll be disturbing his work," Peacock said, smiling.

"I've already discussed this carefully with Constable Wilson and he's happy for me to help him with anything I might learn. He, at least, understands that the police need the public's help and support if they're to succeed."

"That's very true, Miss Riddell," Peacock replied. "Fortunately, many of us share Constable Wilson's understanding. But, I repeat, I'm investigating the murder of your cousin and, as you say, Constable Wilson is investigating the local crime spree. Those are both Police investigations and not something you can interfere with."

"Inspector," Pauline replied, "the will is my focus. I assure you, my only interest in Walter's murder, other than personal obviously, and the incidents is that they may relate to the will." She felt herself blushing a little at the lie. She was sure there was one shadowy entity behind all this and when she'd proven the will a forgery, it would lay bare the murderer. She owed Walter that and she would pay her debt, whatever the cost.

The puzzle of the incidents, however, had led Pauline's thoughts to a difficult place. How could she ask the local bigwig, Frank Thornton, if his brother was a thief. He'd been upset enough when she'd suggested his lawyer was at fault and now she was going to say even worse about his family.

# 8

## SNOWED IN ON BOXING DAY

THE WEATHER HAD TAKEN a turn for the worse overnight and the farm track was buried under deep drifts that looked impassable to her car. Only the farm tractor could reach the road and it didn't have a snowplow. Pauline's mood was torn between relief at not being able to get out to investigate, frustration for exactly the same reason, and annoyance the groceries she'd bought for the family gathering now all had to be eaten by her and her parents for no one could visit this day.

To prevent her mother from going out for the eggs, Pauline put on one of her father's thick coats and his wellington boots and set out for the hen house. At least it was warm in there, she thought, as she battled her way through the blowing snow and drifts that were forming in the yard. She opened the door, stepped inside, and closed it quickly, not wanting to lose any of the delicious heat. After her bedroom and the not yet heated living room, the henhouse felt more like a hot house.

As she gathered the eggs, Pauline thought about her next steps. The best hope of saving the Thornton estate from ruin, and her brother Alan's farm and livelihood with it, was to find that original first page of the will. With luck, Ogilvie may learn something there. She paused in her collecting as another thought struck her. One that she should have thought of before. Surely, the Thornton family must have a copy of it somewhere in the manor. It was inconceivable the only copy was in the solicitor's office. The moment she got back in the house, she'd call Thornton and Ogilvie to ask. This opportunity to further her investigation invigorated her and she finished up the egg collecting in record time. Even the walk back to the house seemed quicker when there was a more interesting object in view.

"Not that I'm aware of, Miss Riddell," Frank Thornton said, when she got him on the phone. "I never knew of one and Dad didn't mention it in the final days. If he did know of one he'd forgotten."

"Or he assumed you knew, or his mind was elsewhere," Pauline said. "I can't believe that when the lawyer drew up the will back in 1945 or whenever, your father wasn't given a copy."

"It does seem odd," Thornton said. "I've been meaning to get stuck into the old papers in the office. Now I'm my own manager, I really should. Today and tomorrow, if the weather forecasts are correct, will be a good time to do that."

Her call to John Ogilvie was equally unsatisfactory. "I wasn't there at the time, Miss Riddell," he said in answer to her question about whether a copy had been given to the Thorntons. "Nowadays, of course, with modern photocopying machines, we always give a copy but back then, I don't know. I would think they would. I'll see if there's any record of it."

"Would your father, or old Harry, have kept such records?"

"Probably not. As I say, things were done differently then.

Particularly with the Thorntons. We weren't just lawyer and client, we were, and I hope still are, friends."

"I understand. It's odd how we treat our friends with so much less consideration than we do those we don't care about."

"It's true, sadly. On a more cheerful note, I take it from this call you're still thinking about our problem. Have you any other plans in mind for when we can move around again?"

"I wish I had. It frustrates me no end that we can't get the will to a better-equipped lab because of this awful weather."

"I agree. Every time the phone rings I expect it to be Anthony Thornton demanding to know when the will is to be read."

"Your imaginary flu must be wearing off," Pauline agreed. "I think Frank Thornton may have to catch it now."

"That may gain us another week but not much more."

"Which is why a copy of the will would be good to find. Have you thought of calling the beneficiaries of old Harry's will?"

"I did. Harry left everything to a second cousin. Harry was a bachelor you know, but the cousin's visiting family for the holidays and won't be back until after the New Year, or so his housekeeper says."

"This vacationing from Christmas Eve until after New Year's Day is the curse of the modern age," Pauline grumbled, ignoring her own regular use of vacation days to do just that. "Our competitors around the world must think we're mad."

"It doesn't do we poor seekers after truth any good either," Ogilvie said. "Now I must go. The children are demanding to be amused and I can hear my wife wondering what it is I can be doing that is keeping me away so long."

Having set the two men searching for documents, Pauline

returned to the kitchen to help her mother wash and pack eggs, her mind now centered on the problem of Walter's murder. She was still pondering it when she and her parents pulled up chairs around the fire with a sherry and mince pie. Considering her parents were practically teetotalers, they drank a surprising amount of sweet spirits at Christmas time.

# 9

# FORGED BUT GENUINE WILL – DECEMBER 27

AFTER CUDGELING her brain for days, Pauline couldn't think of a good way of suggesting to Frank Thornton his brother was a scoundrel. So, with her brother as local cover and also as four-wheel drive driver, she traveled over to the manor on the following day, when the roads had been partially cleared, with the intention of just bluntly asking. The master of the house answered the door and ushered them into a comfortable room, well heated by a log fire, where he indicated they should take seats.

"Can I get you anything to drink?" Thornton asked. "I've no staff here today, as you see. I'm not sure there'll ever be staff here again, but I thought they should stay at home with their families during this awful weather over Christmas."

"Nothing for me," Pauline said. "I only came to follow up on some things I've heard that you might be able to explain. Then we'll be on our way before today's snow grows even worse."

Alan, taking his lead from her, also declined any refreshment.

"What is it you wanted to ask?"

"The incidents that were happening and the forged will seem unrelated but we, Alan and I, don't see how they can be," Pauline said. "After all, none of these things or anything like them have happened before. I don't want to point fingers but your brother, Anthony, was famous for the bad company he kept. I know he's no longer around, but could there be someone here with whom he's still friendly and who might do some or all of these things on your brother's say so?"

"My brother had few friends in this neighborhood and has even fewer since he moved away," Frank Thornton said.

"So you can't think of anyone who would be willing to risk forging the will or playing pranks on people, perhaps with the idea of distracting from the forgery until it was too late?" Pauline asked.

"No one. To be honest, he only had one friend here that I know of and he was a bad lot too."

"In what way?"

"He was always up to mischief, and now I think of it, these incidents were exactly the sort of thing he would have done."

"Surely something was done about him at the time?"

"He was a clever little rogue and such an attractive boy, looked like an angel people said, no one had the heart to do anything. And to be fair to everyone, there was never any real proof it was him. Just everyone knew it was. And everyone was sorry for his father. He'd lost his wife to illness when the boy was small, but he seemed to cope well. He was a hard worker; everyone liked him, so you see no one wanted to bring down even more grief on him by accusing his son without solid evidence."

"Is the boy, man now, still here? Could he be behind these incidents?"

Thornton shook his head. "Neville Duck? No. He left

years ago, before the war, and hasn't been seen or heard of since. Apparently, his father also believed he was behind all the spiteful pranks of the day and they had a big falling out. Neville's father, by the way, was our estate's gamekeeper. He was a good man, well respected by everyone, who sadly died a few years later. Heartbroken, everyone says."

"You have no idea where the boy went?"

"None at all," Thornton said. "To be honest, I just thought it was a good thing for his father and good riddance. I've never given him a second thought until this very moment."

"Alan?" Pauline asked. "This boy must have been about your age. Did you know him?"

Alan shook his head. "He were a bad lot, as Mr. Thornton says. We avoided him. You'll likely think our shunning him was why he was the way he was but it were the other way around. We avoided him because he did bad things and I don't think he grew worse because we kept him at a distance."

"And there's no one else?" Pauline asked, looking from one to the other.

"We're a small community, Miss Riddell, as you know. We have our sinners," Thornton smiled as he said this, "but not the sort who would do what has been done lately. The only one who was that sort was Neville Duck, other than my brother of course."

"I think we should have the police look into where he might be now," Pauline replied. "Whoever's behind these events knows a lot about what goes on in this village. They're not strangers. If there's a chance this man is nearby, we should find out. You are sure your brother isn't anywhere about, aren't you?"

"I am," Frank said. "Here let me show you his letter. It says he's in London. It will also give you a good idea of the kind of man he is."

"When was this letter sent?"

"Back in September. When I knew for sure Dad was dying, I sent Tony a letter urging him to come home and see Dad before the end." Frank left the room, returning moments later with an air mail envelope in his hand. "Read it," he said, handing it to Pauline.

She opened up the letter and read:

*Frank,*

*The old man never liked me, and I hated him. There would be no reconciliation to bring tears to your dutifully sorrowful eyes. I'm coming to London soon for the Season so send the pittance that will be my share of the estate to the bank's London branch. I'll pick it up there and celebrate his passing in style.*

*Tony*

"If this letter is to be believed," Pauline said, "your brother didn't know of the forged will."

Frank snorted derisively. "Of course, he knew. He put that in there so I wouldn't be able to use the letter when I challenge the forgery in court."

Pauline nodded. "I agree," she said, "but a judge would have to take it at face value."

"A sane one wouldn't."

"Do you know if he actually is in London?" she asked.

"Wait," Frank said, and left the room. He returned with a newspaper opened at the society page and handed it to her.

Pauline read the paragraph below the photo Frank pointed to: *The always popular Tony Thornton escorting one of our rising movie starlets to the ball.* She checked the date and confirmed it was only a week earlier. "He's going to be asking where the money from the will is very soon," she said.

"I know but I'm damned if I'll have that will read until we – you -- have exhausted every channel. As you well remember, our plan is to tell him John Ogilvie has this awful flu that's going around and he's not able to work. When that loses its credibility, I'll say I have it."

"That might hold him off for a week or two but not longer."

"And we've used up precious days of that time already by having the police fail to prove the will a forgery."

"Do you know what methods they used to test it?"

Frank shrugged. "They said they confirmed the paper and ink of the pages were consistent with the time and place and with each other. Isn't that enough?"

"Probably," Pauline said thoughtfully. "I wonder if there are any newer, more sophisticated tests available that we could use?"

"Such as?"

"I don't know right now but there are people I've met and worked with on other investigations who would know. By the way, will you call John Ogilvie and tell him I want to search his offices and stockroom?"

"You think you might find old paper and ink in drawers and cupboards?"

"I might but if what I think happened, dear old Harry will have cleared them out after the forgery was made. Still, it's worth a try."

Frank again left the room and returned a few minutes later. "John says you're welcome to look but he thought of that and searched pretty thoroughly when the deception was discovered."

Pauline nodded. "Nevertheless," she said, "a fresh pair of eyes often find things the regular observer misses."

Alan drove Pauline into Goathland to search Ogilvie's premises. She'd said it was worth a try more in hope than genuine belief and so it proved. Ogilvie office's stock of paper and ink was newer than the late nineteen-forties.

"I don't like saying this, Miss Riddell," John Ogilvie said, "but I've come to think you may be right about Harry."

"And what has changed your mind?"

"When I started searching, something I did or saw reminded me that Harry had a big clear-out before he retired. He said his pride required him to hand over the job to the new man in the best shape it could be. At the time, I thought it was just Harry being Harry. He was always a stickler for a place for everything and everything in its place. I suspect now he was destroying the evidence."

"Sadly, for Harry, the person who put him up to it also wanted to destroy the evidence."

Ogilvie looked aghast. "Surely not. You can't be suggesting Anthony Thornton killed Harry?"

"He had a lot to lose if old Harry had a sudden attack of conscience and Harry sounds like the sort of man whose conscience would trouble him."

"But still," Ogilvie said. "Anthony Thornton may be many things but he's a gentleman and what you're suggesting is like something from a gangland turf war. Those Kray twins we read about in the papers might do something like that but a Thornton? Never."

"Maybe he didn't do it himself," Pauline said. "He may have paid others to do it. Would that make it better?"

Ogilvie frowned. "No, Miss Riddell. It would not."

"I'd like to have the will examined by others," Pauline said, changing the subject quickly. "Would it be possible to have it taken to a university or similar laboratory for testing if I can find one that looks into these things?"

"The police examined it."

"I know. I just think they may not have had the latest and best equipment."

"Who would have better?"

"Perhaps a large document archive or library," Pauline

said. "People who regularly test the age of documents for historians, for example. Even a police lab from a big city might have newer equipment."

"Do you have one you wish to try?"

"Not yet. I have some phone calls to make but I'd like you and the will ready to travel the moment I do."

"You have my full support, Miss Riddell. I want this nightmare ended as much as I'm sure Frank and all his staff and tenants do."

Pauline drove home as quickly as she dared on the icy roads, hoping a phone call would find her friend Chief Inspector Ramsay still in his office.

"Chief Inspector," Pauline said, when she heard his usual gruff response to a telephone interruption. "How nice to hear you again."

"Merry Christmas to you too, Miss Riddell," Ramsay said. "It's good to hear from you, though I suspect I'll regret this call as I so often do when you get in touch."

"That's not true, Inspector, and I'll pretend I didn't hear it."

"What is it you want, or did you just call to wish me Season's Greetings?"

"I wouldn't waste your time with nonsense of that sort, Chief Inspector, as I'm sure you know. I wanted to ask about the laboratories the police have in Newcastle or have access to."

"For what?"

"I have a will that I hope some sophisticated equipment can prove is a forgery, or at least part of it is."

"I thought you were on holiday in Yorkshire. Don't they have labs down there?"

"I want big city equipment, not the county bobby stuff."

"I hope you haven't said this to my colleagues down there. People can be touchy about their competence."

"I haven't. Can you help me?" Pauline asked.

"How are you going to get it up here? The snow is bad again today, many roads are closed."

"The first day the roads are clear then."

"Very well. Are you involved with the murder that happened down there?" Ramsay asked.

"Yes and no," Pauline said. "The victim was my cousin and I have an interest, but the police are doing the work. I'm just giving it my best thought."

"If you put a will above a cousin's murder, I have to wonder about that cousin," Ramsay said.

She could hear the amusement in his voice. "I didn't know, because we lost touch when I moved away, but it turns out my cousin had drifted into a life of crime so you can imagine how I feel about him."

"We're none of us responsible for our relations, Miss Riddell," Ramsay said, laughing. "You said yes and no. Does that mean there's something odd about his death. Other than a falling out amongst thieves, I mean?"

Pauline began to explain about the other puzzling things in the locality, when she saw her parents' angry stares.

"I'm sorry, Inspector, this isn't my phone. This call will be costing my parents far more than they can afford. When the weather forecast says it's safe, I'll call again and arrange a time to drive up to Newcastle and we can meet and talk."

She hung up the phone, feeling guilty. She was used to phoning people locally and she could afford it on her salary. A long-distance call on her parents' income would be a real struggle to pay.

"Don't worry," Pauline said, "I'll pay for the call and the others I'll make."

"Maybe you can afford these things on your wages, and not having a family to support," her mother said, "but we find it hard to make ends meet these days. The money has quite gone out of farming."

"The money is going out of everything," her father added. "It's like the war was never over."

Pauline found her purse and quickly handed over a pound note before they began another rambling things-were-so-much-better-when tale.

# 10

## MR. RIDDELL'S INFORMATION – DECEMBER 28

THE WEATHER HAD TURNED wild again by the time Pauline woke next morning. According to the radio, the south and west of the country were being most badly hit but Pauline couldn't see how it could be worse down there. The blizzard was so heavy, she could hardly see the farm buildings across the yard and any thought of getting the eggs was out of the question. How she'd prevail on her mother to agree was another matter.

She rose, hurriedly dressed, and with her mother, cleared out the ashes and re-lit the fires before beginning to make breakfast.

"We'll go together for the eggs," her mother suddenly announced. "It wouldn't be safe for just one of us to go."

"Better to lose two women rather than just one, you think, Mum?"

"Nonsense, Polly. You do talk such rot sometimes. The henhouse is at the bottom of the farmyard not the bottom of the sea."

"Mother," Pauline said. "We can't even see it. If we were there, we couldn't see back here to the house. It would be easy to be lost in that blizzard. The eggs can wait until it clears enough to see our way."

"And your father? Can the cows wait for the weather to clear before he gets the milking machine on them? Or does he just have to take his chances while we put our feet up in front of the fire? This is a farm, lass. Not one of yon offices you work in."

Realizing she was never going to win this argument and loathe to let her mother go outside when she was so recently ill, Pauline said, "Then you stay indoors. I'll go with Dad when he goes out to the cowshed. He can pick me up on his way back. That way no one is alone out there."

Dressed in every piece of clothing they possessed, Pauline and her father made their way to do the farm's morning chores. By the time she'd collected the eggs, and her father had returned to the henhouse from milking the cows, the storm was abating.

"The milk will freeze if it stays like this," her father said, laughing, as he stamped the snow off his shoes and rubbed his hands for warmth.

Pauline, who'd looked out as her father was entering through the door, said, "We can at least see the house now, even if we freeze before we get there." She was well aware the milk was in no danger.

"Aye," he said. "We'll be fine. Meanwhile, we have some time to talk. I don't get much chance when your mother's about. How is your investigation going?"

"As well as it ever does at this stage. Why?"

"You haven't told us much about it and you haven't asked us anything about what's been going on. I thought I'd ask you instead."

"I like to keep my thoughts to myself," Pauline said. "People go off on wild paths if I share my suspicions. They say the wrong things to the wrong people, or they do something silly and make things worse."

"I can see how that might be," her father agreed. "Still, it isn't very flattering of you to assume your mother and I know nothing of what's been going on here."

"Do you know something I should know?"

"We don't know what you don't know, Pauline. We can only know that if you ask us for information."

Not entirely sure if her father was genuinely put out that she hadn't questioned them or whether he was teasing her, Pauline thought it best to play along and asked, "What can you tell me about Walter's doings these past years? I can't believe you were very pleased."

"You believe rightly. I could have murdered him myself, thank you for asking. He's been such an embarrassment to all of us. We're respectable, law-abiding people. We always have been. Having someone like that in the family makes us all look bad."

"So, you don't entirely subscribe to the idea that poaching and smuggling are perfectly understandable wrongdoings? I got the impression you did."

"If someone shoots the odd pheasant or exchanges the odd bottle with a foreigner, that's one thing," her father said. "Making a business out of it is different. But, to your point, we have to laugh it off or we'd just look more ridiculous than we did when he was living among us and brazenly admitting to lawbreaking whenever he had a few too many drinks in him."

Pauline nodded. She could imagine how this would affect someone as honest as her parents saw themselves.

"What can you tell me about his actions, his motives – anything really?"

"His motives were he was a man who couldn't brook

authority so couldn't hold down a job anywhere and had to fall back on the patch of land attached to the cottage he was left by his father. It couldn't sustain anyone, even if he'd made a better effort than he did. I think though, slowly greed took over. His actions were getting bigger and more profitable."

"Then it's only recently he bought new things?"

"The past two years is when he's had more money to spend."

Pauline didn't like the sound of that at all. "Is there anything else?"

"I wondered about the break-ins," her father said. "He never liked old Miss Goforth and he often had run ins with Tom Pringle, the old bobby. And if anyone would know where to sell on stolen goods, it would be your cousin Walter."

"Charming," Pauline said. "A real asset to the family was *my* cousin Walter." She stressed the relationship to gently rebuke her father before adding, "But you've no proof of that? It certainly isn't how I remember Walter."

"I haven't any proof and him getting his head bashed in might suggest he didn't do any of the robberies or unpleasant incidents but was in fact the next victim."

"I doubt burglars would imagine Walter was flush with cash," Pauline said.

"People talk and Walter boasted a lot in his cups so it's possible someone thought he was worth burgling. It's also possible he fell out with his accomplices."

"Leaving our own black sheep of the family for a moment, what can you remember about Anthony Thornton?"

"He was a bad un, that one. Right from the off. Some bairns are that way and they grow out of it but not him."

"What kind of bad things are we talking about?"

"Cruelty to small animals and other children, mainly. You know the kind of things they do. I'm sure you can think of

64

some in the village school when you went there who were a bit that way."

Pauline nodded, she could indeed. "And when he was older?"

"He took up with the Duck boy, who was another one you had to watch. You couldn't leave anything lying around if he was nearby," he paused, then added, "nor leave any small creature with him either. He and Tony Thornton were a real couple, in so many ways."

"If people knew this, why was nothing done?"

"Common enough reasons: misplaced loyalty and sympathy. One was the son of the local landowner, we all pay our rents to him, and the other was, well, he was different and everyone felt sorry for his father who was widowed when the boy was small."

"And everyone hoped for the best."

"Exactly, because as I said, most children grow out of these things," her father said. "And they both did seem to get better as they matured. I'm not saying we didn't have suspicions, only there was never any proof when they were older. Personally, I think they'd just grown wise enough to cover their tracks, but I have a very dim view of human nature."

"It was an odd combination," Pauline said, "the squire's son and the gamekeeper's son as a gang of juvenile delinquents."

"Mebbe. But it were so. As I said, they had tastes in common."

A thought that had been in her mind for days, came out. "Is Anthony Thornton married?"

"We heard he'd married a refugee from Tunisia or Algeria, one of them places the French have just been kicked out of. It was years ago, right when the trouble was starting. We've never seen her, mind. They live in the house he has in the south of France and he's never brought her here. When he comes here, as he does every few years to remind us he's as dissolute as ever, he brings floozies from London. That place must be full of them, the numbers he finds."

"No one wearing the Arab gowns and veil then," Pauline asked mischievously.

"No one wearing much at all," her father said, "from what I hear. That's hearsay, by the way. I didn't witness any of the goings-on. Sadly, I don't get invited to those kinds of parties," he paused, wistfully it seemed to Pauline, and then added, "but his wife probably wouldn't wear Arab dress, would she? If she was a refugee, I mean. She'd be French."

"True. I wasn't being serious. I did wonder if the woman artist might have been his wife."

"Aye, we thought that too but why was she here alone and why now, after all these years?"

"That I can't answer," Pauline admitted. "Still, it has to be a possibility."

"We should be getting back," her father said, "or your mother will come looking for us and you know what the doctor said."

They wrapped their coats, hats and collars against the wind and stepped outside. The wind was as sharp as a knife, cutting through all Pauline's clothes, chilling her to the marrow.

"Where have you been?" Mrs. Riddell greeted them as they burst through the kitchen door into the warmth.

"Waiting for the storm to die down," Pauline said.

"It did that hours ago," her mother said. "Well, don't just stand there. Get your coats off and get in near the fire. I'll bring you a hot drink in a minute."

Knowing she would fuss if she wasn't allowed to have her way, Pauline and her father did as they were told.

When they were all seated around the fire, Pauline said, "Mum, I'd wondered if the Frenchwoman artist mightn't have been Anthony Thornton's wife. Dad thought not. What do you think?"

"I have no idea, Polly. We did wonder but she didn't call herself Thornton. She had a French name, Mrs. Drayton says. It was on the letters she received. What was it? Oh, dear. My memory. Mrs. Drayton would know. Phone her and ask."

"I will. I just find it odd, her coming here I mean," Pauline said. "I understand Thornton recommending it. He would get some rental income, but I find it hard to believe she'd come. After all, artists go where other artists go. The last thing they want is to paint pictures of somewhere other artists haven't already approved of."

"Isn't art supposed to have some measure of originality in it?" her mother asked.

"If it is, then there's even less art around than I thought," Pauline said, grinning. "Landscapes, in particular, come in sets, like cutlery – there's beach, forest, hills, lakes, and mountain scenes. I've never seen the moors."

"Maybe he misrepresented the scenery to her?"

"Surely not," Pauline said, laughing, "and him such an upright man."

"But, if she's someone he knows back at his French home, he would be damaging himself by lying to her," her mother said thoughtfully. "It's very tangled, isn't it? Imagining what and why people have done unusual things. One never knows what might move someone to do something out of the ordinary."

"One doesn't," Pauline agreed, "which is why I like doing this. Observing people, first-hand, if I can, or secondhand, if I can't, and then piecing together their motivation from what I see. It's better than a jigsaw puzzle."

Her mother laughed. "Do you remember how much we enjoyed doing them?"

"I do."

"I'm sure we still have that big one of the Matterhorn. I know I saw it upstairs just a while ago. Why don't we do it again as we can't get out?"

Mrs. Riddell quickly left the room in search of the puzzle.

"Just don't ask me to help," her father said, grinning. "I want a quiet Christmas."

# 11

## A NEW LINE OF ENQUIRY – DECEMBER 29

NEXT MORNING, after their chores were done, Pauline and her mother continued the jigsaw puzzle, while Mr. Riddell got out the farm tractor and began leveling the snow from the yard to the road. However, he was barely halfway when the storm closed in again and he retired to the house for a late lunch.

"The radio says down south they're dropping food to animals on the open moors," Pauline told her father when he returned.

"I hope they'll do the same here if we have another day like these two," her father said. "We have enough hay and silage to cover short spells where the grass is covered by snow, but the fields have been covered now for a week."

"And we have very few beasts," Mrs. Riddell said. "How folks with bigger herds are getting by, I don't know."

"Changing the subject," Pauline said, "did Walter have any new friends that you know of?"

"Where did this come from," her father asked.

"I was thinking about what you said about him being richer recently and I wondered, did you see or hear of any new friends?"

"Not really," Mrs. Riddell said, looking to her husband for confirmation. "Did you hear of anything like that, Christopher?"

"Walter only had one real friend in these last years," her father said. "That were Sam Tunstall. The rest of us started giving Walter a wide berth years ago."

"What does Sam do?" Pauline asked, praying she wouldn't hear what she'd feared in the cold wee hours of the night.

"He works for a local contractor, called Grounds Keeper, cutting hedges, trees and grass."

Pauline tried not to let her relief show. "I'm surprised Sam didn't get Walter taken on, too," she said. "Surely, that would be a job Walter would like, being outdoors and that."

Her mother laughed. "I doubt he'd get the clearance," she said. "They do the grounds around the early warning station. Just to get in and cut the grass, you have to have MI5, or some such organization, provide you a good reference. Walter was always in court for something or other – not I think the kind of citizen to get security approval."

Pauline insides felt hollow and she practically groaned with frustration. Yet another line of enquiry to follow and this time with no way of following it. Inspector Ramsay may now be a Chief Inspector but he still had no time for the nation's secret services and would never approach them for something as unlikely as this. Even if Walter had been friends with someone who went into the compound around the early warning station, that wouldn't provide him with any way of getting vital information about the equipment or what went on there. Unless, of course, there was a third person inside who passed the information to Sam who passed it to Walter who passed it to the captain of a Russian trawler.

But how plausible was that? In a world where your life depended on keeping everything close, would anyone devise such a loose way of passing on treasonous information? And particularly with characters as notoriously unreliable as Walter and probably his friend, Sam?

"Dad," she said, "could you persuade Sam to talk to me?" Pauline could believe her rascal of a cousin would poach and smuggle but spying for a foreign power? Surely not. Maybe Sam would be able to settle that question and lift the awful fear that was growing in her mind.

"I can ask," her father said, "but he was the one who found Walter and the police have been interviewing him for days so he may not be keen to talk to you."

"Then we'll meet him together," Pauline said. "Where might we do that?"

"The Shepherd's Arms. Like many of the wasters around here, he'll be there most nights of the weekend."

"When the weather improves, we should be there."

"Pauline, other than with my fellow farmers at lunch time on market day, I don't go there. I particularly don't go there in the evening. If you turned up as well as me, the place would shut up. No one would say a word."

"Then find somewhere, Dad, because I need to know all he can tell me about his time with Walter."

## 12

# MORE REVELATIONS – DECEMBER 30

NEXT MORNING, while her father was finding a way for her to interview Sam Tunstall, Pauline took the opportunity to go with her mother, aunts, and other local family members to begin clearing Walter's cottage of his personal items. As one of many, Pauline was able to search her dead cousin's home without raising any eyebrows. It was, however, a disappointing morning for both Pauline and the other women. Being an old bachelor, Walter had few items that would be an asset in their homes. The most lucrative item was the coal in the coalhouse, which was meticulously shared into buckets and scuttles to be carried off when the men came to collect them all at lunch time.

As her father brought them home in the four-wheel drive, he told Pauline that Sam would likely be in the Shepherd's Arms at lunch time. The Grounds Keepers company had snow removal contracts at many businesses and the pub was one of them. He couldn't believe Sam Tunstall, if he was half as sharp as was advertised, would not have scheduled his part of the work to take place at the pub near lunch time. Without waiting for her own lunch, Pauline jumped in her car and headed out.

Her father was not wrong. Entering the bar, she saw a group of men in high-visibility jackets, laughing and joshing each other around a long table. They fell quiet the moment they saw her but not before she'd heard one of them addressed as Sam.

"Are you Sam Tunstall?" she asked the man. He was a burly man, graying at the temples and not well-shaved.

"Who's asking?" he replied.

"I'm Pauline Riddell. You know my parents Christopher and Doris Riddell and you knew my cousin Walter. I wondered if we could talk about Walter for a few minutes."

"Why?"

"Well, he was my favorite cousin when we were children," Pauline said. "He always thought of clever things to do. And because I would like to know what happened to him and the police won't tell me anything."

"Then I don't think I should either."

Seeing this wasn't getting anywhere fast, Pauline decided to appeal directly to his better nature. "I'm not rich but I could buy you a drink for your trouble," she said.

"That's more like it," he said. "Mine's a Glenfiddich. Working outside on a cold day like this, you need a wee dram of scotch inside you to keep warm."

"Very well," Pauline said. "I'll get the drinks and we'll sit at the table by the fire." She nodded toward the fireplace where a roaring fire threw out waves of heat she could feel even at the back of the room.

Handing him his drink, and sitting across the small table from him, Pauline asked, "Can we start with the night you found poor Walter's body?"

He recounted the events, while she studied his face for signs of evasion. It seemed genuine so when he finished, she asked, "Were you and Walter coming here that night or did you have some other jaunt in mind?"

"What are you asking?" he demanded.

"I'm not the police. If you were going poaching, for example, I wouldn't need to mention that to anyone. It's not like it's a crime."

"No sense poaching with two feet of snow on the ground," he said contemptuous of anyone who didn't understand even the basics of country life.

"I only used that as an example," Pauline said. "I understand Walter did some free trading as well."

"The weather's been so bad lately, there's no boats out there now."

"Did you know the people Walter sold his free traded goods on to?"

"Nay, lass. We were just drinking mates, really. Nowt like that come up in conversation."

She was being much too direct, she knew, but decided to continue. "You never saw him with anyone you didn't recognize? Someone from out of the district?"

"I didn't say that," he said, indicating his glass was already empty and putting on the expression of a poor working man who desperately needed to keep out the cold.

Pauline sighed and went to the bar for another. She only hoped he wasn't operating any of the snowplows she'd seen parked outside the door.

"There were someone," he said, when she delivered his refill. "A middle-aged man, sharp dresser, city folk. I told the police, too. I guess it was him that did it."

"Did you get a license plate number or something useful like that?"

"Nay, lass. They were too far away and I wasn't interested. At the time, I thought it was just someone asking directions. That's what Walter told me when I asked. It was only after the murder I put it all together."

"Walter wasn't responsible for those burglaries, was he?" Pauline asked.

"Walter were an honest man," Sam said. "Pheasants are wild creatures and belong to everyman and free trading is what governments are always saying they want for us all, so that can't be wrong either. Stealing from folk is not what the likes of Walter were about."

"Do you have any ideas about the robberies?"

"Nay, why should I?"

"You live here, and through Walter, must have heard what is being said in low voices."

"Walter thought it were yon Frenchwoman," Sam said.

"Why did he think that?"

"He saw her out and about after dark, he said."

"That is interesting. I wouldn't have thought she would know her way about well enough to wander around in the dark."

"Oh, she were a great one for walking. Everyone up on the moors would see her sitting at her easel painting or just walking with her camera, looking for things to paint, they say."

"I expect so," Pauline agreed. "And if she was always out and about, perhaps she did know enough to walk there in the dark, as you say. I expect she was looking for moonlit scenes."

"Probably," Sam said, turning to nod to the other men who were preparing to leave. "Got to go, miss," he said. "Sorry I couldn't help you more with Walter."

"One last thing, did you ever go with him to meet the trawler crews in Whitby or Scarborough?"

He shook his head. "I don't hold with foreigners, not even if they are free traders," he said, and left.

# 13

## NEW YEAR'S EVE

THE FOLLOWING DAY, Pauline set out to keep her watch at the Dower house. She parked her car on the snow-covered street and, when she was sure no one was watching, walked quickly down the track to her observation post. Many people in the north took New Year's Eve as a holiday but she thought it likely the estate agent wouldn't. What she saw was exactly what she had expected. A sullen-looking youth, who barely looked old enough to drive, drove up the lane at the back of the old house. He examined the house from the car while he smoked a cigarette. She thought his duties weren't so pressing on him that a cold wind and hard frost wouldn't prevent him from carrying them out.

She was wrong. When the cigarette was finished, he got out of the car and made his way through the gate and up the path to the back door of the house. He peered in at the kitchen window before unlocking the door and entering.

Pauline, shivering in the evergreen bushes that separated the lane from the fields behind, watched and waited. Time passed slowly. She was just beginning to think he'd fallen asleep in the house when he re-emerged and returned to his car. He made some notes on a clipboard and then drove off.

For Pauline, this was the moment when she hoped to see any illicit squatter in the house return but nothing happened. After an hour, with her fingers and toes numbed, she left her hiding place and set off back along the lane to the road. She'd investigated this lane before, hoping to see evidence of footsteps that she could follow in the snow but there'd never been a clear enough set to follow. Today was no different, the blizzard on the day after Christmas Day, and the continued heavy snowstorms since, had wiped out everything and there was only a jumbled trail through the snow, the young man's prints on top.

She called in at the police house on her return to ask Constable Wilson if he'd had any new leads on the robberies. That it might also give her some time in a warm house to thaw out before she walked back to Alan's farm was an added attraction.

She did get to thaw out a little for Mrs. Wilson was happy to have such an illustrious visitor in her sitting room, but she didn't hear any new information.

"Nay, Miss," Constable Wilson said, in reply to her gentle probing questions, "even if I were allowed to tell you anything, I couldn't, for we have nothing new to say."

"That is disappointing," Pauline said. "You don't think my cousin Walter was a victim of this burgling vandal, do you? He didn't come home early that night and run right into the intruder?"

"We don't think so, Miss," Wilson said. "I can't say what Inspector Peacock and his detective team might think."

"And there have been no new incidents," Pauline said, wondering aloud, hoping to spur the constable on to further speech. "If poor Walter wasn't one of them, then it's been a while, over two weeks, since the last burglary."

"Aye, but the burglar got away with a lot of stuff in that

raid," Wilson said. "I reckon he could live a good few months on that haul."

"True," Pauline agreed, "and if it is someone working on their own, for themselves, that may be enough. I'd had ideas it may be a city gang targeting rural homes for profit, rather than a desperate lone criminal."

"To go out in this weather," Mrs. Wilson said, "they'd need to be desperate, I would think."

"Indeed, for an individual it would be risky. Though a gang would have things organized and each could support the other if things went wrong," Pauline said, still hoping to ease the policeman into an indiscretion.

"Ladies," Wilson said, "there's no question of a big gang involved. The loot that's carried off is no more than one man could carry. And there's never any evidence of more than one person involved."

"Then you're probably thinking the thief and the loot is still in the neighborhood, Constable," Pauline said.

"Likely, miss, but as I say, I couldn't really say."

"Very proper," Pauline agreed. "It wouldn't be right. Well, I must be going or they'll send out a search party for me. I told them I was only going to the post office but the day is so nice, now the snow has stopped, I took the opportunity to stretch my legs by coming here."

Pauline headed back to the farm. The sky was darkening again, and she had a drive up and down the steep sides of the dales to get back to her parents over narrow winding roads covered in beaten down icy snow, which sometimes made her car feel like a sleigh. Today, she wanted to be back before darkness and a new fall of snow made things worse.

Despite her trepidation over the drive, however, she was happier than when the day began. Her theory about an illicit lodger at the Dower house wasn't unproven by them not appearing; it just meant they stayed out longer than they needed to after the estate agent's boy had left. And while Constable Wilson had no new information to impart, he had given her much to think on about the old burglaries: 'no more than one person could carry', he'd said.

The drive home was as scary as she'd thought it might be. Snow was falling heavily, and the roads were treacherous. At every uphill the car fishtailed, no matter how lightly she pressed on the accelerator, and every downhill, no matter how gently she pressed the brakes, was a toboggan ride with the very real chance of leaving the road altogether at the bottom.

After their evening meal, Pauline and her parents drew up their chairs in front of the fire, switched the radio, known locally as the wireless, from the popular music of the day, where a yodeling Australian was remembering someone, to the BBC's light music station and settled down to read.

Before they could begin, Pauline said, "Mum, Dad, I have a question about cousin Walter and I don't want you to fly off the handle because you think I shouldn't think such things about our own flesh and blood."

"We always encouraged you to be curious, Pauline," her mother said. "Why would we be any different about this?"

Since recovering, her mother had been more her usual self, Pauline noted wryly.

"I understand Walter was known to sell contraband goods he'd bought from the foreign trawlermen," Pauline began, "but could he have been selling something to them in exchange?"

"Nay, lass," her father said. "What would Walter have to sell? Some dead pheasants is about all he could manage."

"You've never seen him with money, more money than he should have had?"

"Sometimes, but you'd expect that. He enjoyed a bit of a

flutter on the dogs and horses and even the perennially unlucky have winnings occasionally," her mother said.

"And he did all right when the Frenchies brought in brandy," her father said. "Why?"

"There are Russian trawlers too," Pauline said, "and they may pass on more than just vodka."

"What could Walter have that Russkies could want?" her father asked.

"Information from Fylingdales. The early warning station is right there in Walter's backyard," Pauline said.

"But he didn't work there. Hardly anybody here does, except one local company cuts the grass on the Ministry property."

"But people who do work there must meet people who live here and someone who had made the connection between smuggling goods and foreign ships might go out of their way to bring in an accomplice," Pauline said. "Everybody knew Walter met foreign trawlermen for illicit drink and cigarettes and no one would suspect that other things were being exchanged at the same time."

"Walter was no spy," her father said. "He may have been a bit of a rogue, but he wouldn't betray his country."

"He may not have known what he was doing. A man might give him a package to give to a Russian captain and he might receive a package in return, which he delivered back to the man. He needn't even have known the man's connection to Fylingdales."

"You haven't said this to anyone else, have you?" her father asked. "I don't want us to be pointed out as possible foreign agents."

"Of course, I haven't. Not even to the police, who don't seem to have thought of it for themselves -- yet. But they might and I wanted to know if there's any reason for suspicion."

Her parents gazed at each other and their expression suggested a great deal of thinking and remembering was going on inside their heads.

"We were all surprised when Walter bought that van he has," her mother said slowly.

"True," her father said. "And that big television set. Long before many better off people in the district even had a TV."

Her mother laughed. "And before we could even get programs reliably to watch on it, too," she said. "We didn't get the new transmission tower until late last year."

"That's right. He said he'd won the football pools for that."

"He invited us all to see that transatlantic broadcast they did over that satellite, Telstar. Do you remember that, Pauline? Last summer, I think it was."

"I remember reading about it." Pauline's view of television was not kind and having it being beamed in from a too modern place so far away, lowered her opinion even further.

"That shotgun he had wasn't cheap either," Mrs. Riddell said. "You commented on it at the time."

"Aye, I did. It weren't one of the regular guns we all have. Quite special as I recall. I never seen it again."

Pauline's heart sank. She had to alert Peacock to this possibility.

"Who is going to approach the bank about Walter's account, if he had one?" she asked.

"Oh, I doubt he had one," her father said. "He always said banks were thieves and hand-in-glove with the police, who were worse,"

"Then we need to search his house really thoroughly before it's sold," Pauline said. "Not just divvy up his old clothes and crockery."

"You're right there, lass," her father said. "I'll ask his

mother for the key. Say I loaned Walter something and need to find it, summat like that."

"Make it something sensible, Dad. We can't afford to raise any suspicions. But if we find piles of cash, we have to tell the police."

"I'll do it tomorrow first thing," he said. "I assume you want to be there?"

"I certainly do," Pauline said. "I want to search every inch of that place before the police decide to search it again."

"They searched after the murder," her mother reminded her.

"But they were looking for weapons and motives, not necessarily items that shouldn't be there, like pots of money."

"If I get the key in the morning, are we going straight there?"

"As soon as we can," Pauline said. "I'm going to meet with Constable Wilson tomorrow morning first thing so phone there if you have the key. I'll meet you at Walter's cottage."

With this decided, the three settled down to a quiet evening of music and books. The time passed in companionable silence until the radio reminded them that New Year was approaching. Her mother topped up their glasses and brought in a plate of mince pies and Christmas cake to nibble on as they waited for the familiar strains of *Auld Lang Syne* and the chimes of Big Ben from London.

There was one bright side to the weather, Pauline thought, as she toasted the passing of 1962 and the start of a new year. No one was 'first footing' in the dale this New Year's Eve, which suited her very well. The thought of a stream of tall, dark-haired men wandering into the house expecting a whisky from the man of the house, and a kiss from the woman, may have been exciting when she was fifteen and setting out on adult life, but now it was enough to make her want to hide under her bed. By the time they'd arrived at her home, the men had usually 'first-footed' at a half-dozen other houses and they were sometimes too merry to be respectable. Instead, thanks to the weather, she and her parents could welcome the New Year with sherry and a mince pie, before jumping into their beds by quarter past the hour. It was bliss!

# 14

# NEW YEAR'S DAY – JANUARY 1, 1963

DESPITE IT BEING a holiday for most, Mrs. Wilson didn't seem annoyed when she opened the door and saw Pauline bundled like an Egyptian mummy in her winter woolens. "Come in, dear. Joe's been expecting you."

Pauline stepped inside and waited until the door was shut before saying, "I'm sorry I'm late but the weather is awful. I thought of phoning to cancel but decided not to."

"Oh, you're not so very late," Mrs. Wilson said. "This way."

She ushered Pauline into the house's 'best' room, the one northern folk only used when important visitors arrived. Pauline was pleased to see a glowing fire in the grate for often these rooms were cold from lack of use.

Constable Wilson stood to greet her. "You wanted to talk," he said, "about the incidents and burglaries."

"I did. Can we go over the events together? I want to be sure I have the dates and activities correct."

Wilson opened his notebook and flipped the pages back to around the middle. "The first, ignoring the shoplifting at the post office, which I think really was kids, was October thirteenth. Poor old Miss Goforth's pet cat was hanged outside her door. She only discovered this when she was leaving the house the following morning to find her."

"That was the only thing that happened on that occasion?"

"Yes, but it was practically a death sentence for the old woman; she was so upset she was taken to hospital by neighbors. You might remember how she doted on her pets, even as a younger woman."

Pauline did remember. Miss Goforth had been the butt of many jokes from herself and her friends when they were growing up. She seemed ancient to them, retired, living alone, with a house full of old souvenirs brought back from around the world by her seafaring brother. He hadn't married either. It seemed to make the whole thing funnier to the local children, she remembered. She shuddered. The knowledge of her own complicity in this tale of misery for the old woman, whose only solace was her pet, made her insides ache with grief.

"I do remember, with great shame," Pauline said.

Wilson nodded. "We all feel the same," he said. "It can't be mended."

It couldn't. Miss Goforth had died at home, alone, only three short weeks after her cat.

"The second?"

"This one was in early November, the fourth. Old Tom Pringle, who'd been the local policeman here before me, had his house burgled. His war medals and his police medals were stolen and much of his personal effects, particularly relating to his late wife, were destroyed."

"The medals turned up in a bin, I understand?"

"Some did. Others were crushed to pieces and dropped on the street through the village."

"Both these were very specifically malicious, just plain spite on somebody's part. Did you have any suspicions?"

"I looked into all the current crop of youngsters at first

and found nothing. Then I checked back ten years, when Tom was still the copper here. I didn't find anything there either."

"Did you look further back?"

"Nay. Even if someone had held a grudge further back, why would they suddenly start to act on it now?"

"There could be reasons, though I agree I can't think what or why," Pauline said. "I just wondered if anyone had returned to the village before the events began."

Wilson shook his head. "I thought of that but there was no one. The only new person in the whole place was yon French-woman staying at the Dower house and it's hard to see how she would even know who the two victims were, let alone have a grudge against them."

"Yet it must have been someone with a grudge," Pauline said, with a frown. "What was next?"

"December thirteenth, the Randall's house was burgled. Now this was a change because the Randalls are relatively new in the village and there was no maliciousness involved. It was a straight old-fashioned burglary."

"What was taken?"

"Money, jewelry, and other small saleable items. Very much a haul of an opportunist type of intruder. And that's what it was. The Randalls had gone away for the weekend and left a window open downstairs."

"Again, this might suggest children if not for the loot. How would children know where to sell on jewelry, for example."

"Exactly. My thinking was still trending toward young-sters, though with an open mind, when the next burglary happened. December eighteenth. This time it was silverware, real stuff, not plate. Do you remember the Coulsons?"

"Yes, but they were old when I was a child."

"They long since died and left everything to their daugh-ter, who was probably away nursing when you were young."

"I remember now. They did have a daughter and as you say not often there."

"She retired back here to live some years ago. She was at home when it happened but she's as deaf as a post and heard nothing. She didn't realize she'd been robbed until midway through the following day."

"This changed your view?" Pauline asked.

"Yes. The first two are different and could be local ne'er-do-wells, Even the third could be them but the fourth needs some kind of vehicle to shift the stuff. I don't mean in the robbery. I mean in getting it away and to a known fence who would take it. It's different."

"I agree," Pauline said. "Have you made any progress with these?"

"Not really, though I'm still working on it. I also keep close links to Inspector Peacock in case your cousin was a victim of the burglar's last robbery."

"I asked the inspector if he thought they were linked and he says they haven't ruled it out but for now they're assuming it was a murder and not a robbery gone horribly wrong. Nothing was taken, as I'm sure you know."

"Aye, I do. So, Miss Riddell, what light can you shed on these events?"

"I thought the Frenchwoman might be the thief," Pauline said. "The two robberies seemed to occur when she was still here. I'm told she was fit, walking the moors every day, and I thought that might make her capable of climbing into windows et cetera. However, it wouldn't explain the spitefulness of the two earlier incidents or the murder of my cousin."

"And having so many incidents in such a timeframe is unlikely to be three different people, resentful kids for the first two, the visitor for the second two, and a third person for the murder," the constable said.

"Exactly. Two maybe, someone learning about the first

ones and using them to cast suspicion elsewhere for the second two or three."

"But murder without theft? Surely, they would take something even if it was just to continue the deception."

"Had you any suspicions about the Frenchwoman, Constable?"

"None. Why would I? She wouldn't know any of the parties involved because she took little part in village life in the short time she was here. She wouldn't know Miss Goforth, who despite her name never went out. She wouldn't know Tom from his working life and she wouldn't know what was to be stolen in the two houses that were robbed."

Pauline nodded. "Yet no one who does know all of those things appears to have done it," she said. "You didn't check to see if she really was a Frenchwoman, did you? Could she have been an English woman who did know the village from years ago and wanted to remain unknown?"

"I'll look into that. If she was who she said she was, she'll have shown her papers when she landed here from France."

"It will also tell us when she arrived in this country and when she left," Pauline said.

"It will be a day or so before I get word," Wilson said.

"Maybe then I'll have some other ideas we can pursue," Pauline said, rising from her chair. "For now, I'll let you get on, constable. I have shopping to do."

Pauline left the police house and walked back to her car deep in thought. It was a puzzle to see how this spate of unpleasantness in the neighborhood linked together. Pulling at each strand didn't seem to help link them at all. And yet, linked she was certain they must be.

When she arrived back at the farm, her father jingled the keys to Walter's cottage to show his success.

"We should go and search now," Pauline said, preparing to head right back out again.

"Not until after lunch," her father said. "We'll all search better on a full stomach. Your mum has it all ready."

Though she was anxious to begin, she had to acknowledge there was truth in that and sat down to eat.

When they arrived at the cottage it was freezing cold. There'd been no fire lit in the place for days now and the cold was in everything they touched. They began work without even taking off their coats and gloves. After an hour of this numbing work, the door opened and a visitor arrived.

"Inspector Peacock," Pauline said, "how nice to see you and Happy New Year. I hope you haven't come to impound all Walter's belongings. Without a will, the family have disposed of the remains equitably and to everyone's satisfaction, as you see." Pauline swung her hands around the empty rooms to illustrate her point. "We're just tidying the last remnants."

"Happy New Year to you too, Miss Riddell," Peacock replied. "I haven't come to impound anything. We searched and took anything that seemed like evidence on the day of the murder. I was just passing and saw your car."

"Then it was me you want to see," Pauline said. "I'm glad. I felt it was time we talked again."

"Do you have something new to say?"

"You first," Pauline replied. "You've just said you wanted to see me, remember?"

Peacock grinned. "I simply wanted to go over what I knew with you and learn anything new you might have learned. Between us, I thought we might unearth something that one of us hasn't yet seen."

"Let me get my hat," Pauline said. "We can walk and talk outside where we won't bother everyone else." The last thing she wanted was the police becoming inquisitive about why they were searching so minutely into nooks and crannies, under loose floorboards and behind walls.

When Pauline was ready, they left the house and began walking slowly along the unplowed lane where deep snow threatened to fall into Pauline's ankle-boots at every step.

"So, you still have evidence of only one intruder," Pauline said. "Yet that intruder carried Walter, who was not a small man, out onto the moor in deep snow and on uneven ground."

"It turns out it doesn't have to be a particularly strong man," Peacock said, "if that's what you're thinking. Your cousin had been ill apparently and was quite thin at the time of his death. Skin and bone, the pathologist says."

"Oh, no one mentioned an illness."

"I think he may have been avoiding people," Peacock said. "We've found very few people who'd seen him much before this happened."

"Poor Walter. He was always a bit eccentric. So, a regular man could have done it then."

"Yes, but they dragged him part of the way. Probably because the snow meant Walter could be easily pulled along the ground like a sled."

"So, not even a regular man. Could a woman have done it?"

"We can't say no but I think it unlikely. It still required a fair degree of upper body strength. Now, what have you learned?"

Pauline outlined her thoughts around the possible squatter at the Dower house.

"You haven't actually seen anyone though?"

"No because I'm lodged with my parents and can't get over to Goathland often enough to keep a proper watch."

"I'll have Constable Wilson keep his eyes open too. If there is someone there, it could explain this murder and the burglaries."

"Couldn't you get a warrant to search it? If you believed there might be stolen property there, I mean."

"If I had some evidence of that, yes, but I haven't."

"Could you ask the estate agent's man to take you around tomorrow?"

"I can ask, but you can be sure that if there's stolen goods in the house, the estate agent's man knows about it and it will be gone within minutes of my call. I suppose you think someone should be watching the place from the time I make my request?"

Pauline grinned. "I do but I think it better you call tomorrow morning, the moment they open, to be sure someone is watching the place right up until the time you arrive. I'll happily volunteer to take a shift. I think we can catch this woman red-handed or, just maybe, it might be a certain Neville Duck, a miscreant from this neighborhood who left some years ago. Perhaps you could have his where-abouts looked into while we catch the criminal."

"Who is Neville Duck?" Peacock said, "And why haven't I heard of him until now, if he's such a dangerous character?"

Pauline told him what she'd learned, adding, "And you haven't been told about him because he left here before the war. He's pretty well forgotten."

"Then why would he be here now?"

"Because he and Anthony Thornton were partners-in-crime when they were teenagers and I think it's possible they still are."

Peacock frowned. "After all this time, it seems unlikely," he said, "but I'll get the team onto finding Mr. Duck, in case you're right. And I'll phone the real estate office tomorrow morning when they open. It'll be just after nine, I imagine. I'll have Constable Wilson meet you... Where, Miss Riddell?"

Pauline thought quickly. It couldn't be where she'd hidden the last time for there wasn't enough cover for two and, to be honest with herself, she didn't want to share the glory of her triumph with anyone. It was very wrong, of course, this pride in her abilities, but sometimes the cause of justice and the desire for praise were perfectly aligned, as they were in this case.

"He and I don't need to meet beforehand, Inspector," she said at last. "I'll be at the back of the house from nine am until I see you leave the house or I see someone else leaving the house before you even get there. Have your man at the front but out of sight. I suggest that small spinney of trees about fifty yards along the road. He will see anything suspicious from there and be in calling distance if I need help to apprehend the culprit."

"Do you really think that's where the burglar and the loot are hidden?" Peacock asked.

"I do. In fact, I'm sure of it.

"Who is it you expect to catch, Miss Riddell? Your mysterious Neville Duck?" Peacock asked. "And will it link to my murder?"

Pauline nodded. "Exactly," she said, "Duck or the Frenchwoman. And when we catch our culprit, I fully expect it to complete my investigations by this time tomorrow. When we have him, or her, we'll soon find the link to the will and the murder, though I think it will take some smart police work to tie it all in."

"Are you always so confident of your deductions, Miss Riddell?"

Pauline considered. "I'm not," she said. "This time, however, I am."

"I hope you're right," Peacock said. "I'd like some time with my children before the school vacations are over. This is the best tobogganing winter since I don't know when and I want to share it with my two."

"And I want to get back to my centrally-heated house,

with its nice gas fireplace, and a good book or two before my annual vacation is all lost on police work," Pauline said.

"Until tomorrow then," Peacock said, unlocking the door to his car. He stopped, and said, "As we are exchanging ideas so freely on my investigation, Miss Fisher, I have a thought for you to consider. Maybe the will is genuine. Do you really know how Frank Thornton and his brother stood in their father's eyes? Do you actually know anything about Frank or Anthony Thornton? Have you considered these possibilities?"

Pauline frowned. She had thought these things but everyone she met was sure the will was forged and they seemed good people. Was that enough to base her investigation on?

"I've asked myself these questions, Inspector, and decided the balance of probability lies with the people I know, rather than the ones I don't."

"They all have an interest in the outcome," he reminded her, before getting into his car and driving off.

His comments were sensible and reasonable, which sent Pauline returning to the search in the cottage in a depressed state of mind. She wasn't really hopeful of finding anything in the cottage. After all, a smuggler-cum-poacher would know not to leave incriminating evidence lying around to be found by just anyone, and the police had already been through Walter's things looking for evidence. But it had to be done. She wouldn't be satisfied until she too had learned everything there was to learn about Walter's life in these recent times, even though it was gleaned secondhand from his meager belongings.

She was fortunate that her parents were in such good standing among the family that she, her mother and her father were able to comb every inch, every wall, every floor, every ceiling and the attic and outhouses to find a hidden secret place where money could be stashed, without suspicious relatives in attendance. Pauline had been afraid someone would want to be with them in case something of value turned up. Nothing did. They did find old magazines, and other items that ladies shouldn't see, but money there was none. Breathing a silent sigh of relief, Pauline decided that, unless Peacock also began asking about secret information and links to Fylingdales, she would say nothing.

Walter's tools and other work equipment had been taken away to be sold at auction and the van already sent to a salesroom. Pauline wished she could have searched all those as well, but it was too late.

"It seems there's nothing beyond what he could have earned through his trading," her father said, as they drove home.

"I'm glad of it," Pauline replied. "It's bad enough the police knowing I had a cousin who flouted the normal laws of the land most of his adult life. A spy or a traitor like Burgess or McLean, or even a just go-between between spies, would have been too much."

"Of course," her mother said, "Walter gambled a lot. It's possible the money went almost as quickly as it came."

"Mum, I don't want to even contemplate the idea."

"Very well, dear, but as detectives on TV are always saying, we have to examine all the possibilities."

"Unless Inspector Peacock starts ferreting around, we say nothing! Right?"

"If he does and finds out you were there ahead of him and didn't tell him, he'll suspect you of having some part in all of this yourself," her mother said primly.

"Think of it like our tax return and your eggs and honey sales at the farm gate, my dear," her father said, winking at Pauline. "This is on a strictly need-to-know basis. That's the way to look at it."

# 15

# IT WASN'T HER – JANUARY 2

AFTER A SLEEPLESS NIGHT where her mind trotted around the parable of the Prodigal Son and how angry the decent hard-working son had been to learn his father was planning a feast for the Prodigal and wondering if that's what she was witnessing here in Yorkshire with Frank and Anthony, Pauline rose at dawn. The early start ensured that by nine o'clock she was up, dressed, had done the farm chores, breakfasted, and driven to Goathland. She hid in the same place she'd watched the Dower house from on the previous occasion, only this time she was better prepared. Her feet were wrapped in nylon stockings, woolen socks and a pair of her father's leather work boots. As well as the stockings, her legs were protected by corduroy work pants, two petticoats, and a thick winter skirt. Two blouses, a sweater, and a jacket protected her upper body, a thick woolen scarf her neck and a wool cap, her head. On top of all this, she wore a thick winter coat with a wide collar that she'd lifted around her ears. Her hands were encased in thin gloves – the kind worn to a ball in days gone by – her kidskin gloves, and on top of both, wool mittens.

According to the plan, Peacock was to phone the estate

agents shortly after nine and demand a tour of the premises immediately. Pauline was sure the agent would delay the inspection for as long as possible to allow the loot to be removed. It would be a long, cold wait if nothing untoward happened, but she was sure the squatter, whoever it was, would be escaping the house soon after receiving word from the real estate agent.

Pauline settled down to wait, confident she'd be released from her vigil very soon. The biggest drawback she could now foresee was that in the middle of winter the sun barely rose above the rim of the dale at this time in the morning and the back of the house was still in a dark shadow. The squatter could be well on their way to the gate, and the lane behind, before she was able to identify him or her and would be off down the lane before she could catch them. She wished she hadn't so casually brushed aside the offer of help from the police.

Another drawback she saw now was she was so well bundled against the cold she could barely move, let alone chase criminals. Both these problems, however, faded into nothing as the minutes ticked away into an hour and she realized no one was going to come racing out of the house at all. Her spirits began to fail.

Even wrapped against the cold as she was, by mid-morning her feet and hands were growing numb. She'd expected that once the call was made, there'd be a flurry of activity as the estate agent's boy and the mysterious lodger worked to remove all the evidence of occupation and probably a lot of the stolen property as well. But there was no visitor and no sign of movement in or around the house. Inspector Peacock might forgive her false prophecy, he was warm in the car and then the house, but she doubted Constable Wilson, who'd been given the task of watching the front of the house, would. The poor man must be frozen to the bone by now. She felt like an icicle and she'd come well prepared. Had he?

Pauline had always found the worst part of detecting to be the long periods of watching and waiting. And this was the worst time yet in her career, not only was it excruciatingly dull but Arctic cold as well. Finally, just after 11:00 am, two cars drove up to the back gate, one with Inspector Peacock and the other with the estate agent himself, no sullen youth today. It took all of Pauline's considerable self-discipline not to rush out and beg to be allowed into the warm police car or to follow them into the house, but she maintained her vigil from the firs.

Peacock was being thorough, Pauline decided, as nearly another hour slipped away before the two men exited the house and made their way back to their cars. The estate agent drove off, after a brief conversation with the inspector, which allowed Pauline to finally leave her hiding place and walk with stiff steps to the police car.

"We should get you inside, Miss Riddell," Peacock said, grinning. "I always thought 'blue with cold' was just an expression but you actually are blue."

Pauline nodded and gratefully slipped into the passenger seat as he held the door for her. She knew the car was cold, but it felt deliciously warm to her.

"Nothing?" Peacock asked.

Pauline shook her head, hardly daring to speak in case her teeth chattered so much they broke. "Nothing," she finally managed.

"We'll pick up Wilson on our way," Peacock said, letting the car roll slowly over the snow and back to the road. "Maybe he had more luck."

He hadn't but Pauline already knew this would be the case. The house had been as lifeless as she'd felt for most of the morning. As Constable Wilson seemed inclined to blame

Pauline for his discomfort, they dropped him at his home to warm up while they made for the local pub.

In the pub, with a hot tea rather than a cold beer, Pauline began to thaw out. The cold was replaced by a sense of guilt.

"It seems I was wrong about the Dower house," she said quietly, for there were other customers even in this inclement weather.

"You were," Peacock agreed, "there was no evidence inside of anyone living there recently and I checked very thoroughly."

"I guessed that," Pauline said ruefully.

Peacock laughed. "It was your idea to watch," he said, "so your discomfort is of your own making."

"It had to be done. The robberies and the earlier incidents all took place around the Dower house and there were tracks in the snow when I first reconnoitered."

"And you still may have been right, Miss Riddell," Peacock said. "After all, a single person living there wouldn't have needed a lot of cleaning up after and it's been a week since your cousin was murdered."

"You agree with me that's a possibility as well?"

"Of course. But even if that wasn't the case, it only means the mysterious maker of tracks had cleared up after themselves and left days ago."

Relieved he didn't seem to be about to give her a tongue-lashing for wasting his and the constable's time, as she feared he might, Pauline said, "Is there any way you could confirm Anthony Thornton is actually in London?"

"You think he's involved?"

"He has to be. It's the only way it makes sense."

"The robberies can't be him. That newspaper column talked about him being at a ball in London on the exact same night one of the break-ins occurred here."

"Maybe not the robberies and maybe not even Walter's death but somehow that will is at the bottom of all this."

Peacock laughed. "You do realize you've just said he isn't involved in all of this and he is involved in all of it in one sentence, don't you?"

Pauline smiled. "I know. I don't see how he's involved in the other two things but I'm sure they're linked somehow. And, if they are, he's at the bottom of it."

"Do you know him?"

Pauline shook her head. "I would have been only about five when he left the neighborhood, and our families weren't in the same social circles. You're asking why I don't like him?"

"That's right. You do seem to have him as the source of all evil."

"Not all evil," Pauline said, "just the source of these recent events. The reason is simple: people I trust don't like him. And he plans to destroy this beautiful landscape by selling it to developers, who are people I really don't like, and I'm told he lived out the war in Vichy, France. I can't forgive any Briton who would do that."

"The root of all evil," Peacock said, still grinning. "But putting your prejudices aside, the only actual reason to believe he is involved is the disputed will and, so far as those who've seen it can tell, it's genuine and he didn't even forge that."

"But to imagine these three events or string of events happening in this small village all in the same short time frame is highly unlikely," Pauline said.

"Wasn't it Sherlock Holmes who said 'when you have eliminated the impossible, whatever remains, however improbable, must be the truth'? And while we haven't entirely eliminated the forgery, or Anthony Thornton being responsible for at least one of the robberies, or him being in the neighborhood when your cousin was killed, we're quite close to doing all of those things. Which leaves us with the improbable being the truth; it's a series of coincidences."

"*When* we have eliminated *all* those things, I'll agree with you, Inspector."

"Well, to be honest, I won't be certain until we've done all that either."

"Then you will find out if Anthony Thornton has been in London this whole time?"

"I'll check with the London police," Peacock said. "I'm sure they'll have a good idea what a dissolute character like him is doing much of the time."

"Ha!" Pauline said. "You don't like him either."

"I don't like what I've heard about him but I don't really know him, so I'll reserve my judgement until he gets here."

"Why do you think he will come?"

"Because, he'll want to know why the will isn't being read, particularly if it is a forgery."

Pauline smiled. "We think alike, Inspector. I too think he'll be here quite soon."


ARRIVING BACK AT HER PARENTS' farm, she promptly called her boss at work to arrange taking one of her 1963 holiday weeks off. It meant forgoing half her yearly vacation, but it couldn't be avoided. As things stood, she had to be back at work within days and the case wasn't even close to being solved.

Her request was granted grudgingly. It was the start of a new year and the work that had piled up over the Christmas and New Year break couldn't wait forever. Promising to work evenings and weekends to get caught up when she returned won her boss over and she hung up the phone with a sigh of relief. That at least had gone right on this disappointing day.

"You seem low tonight, Pauline," her mother said. "I hope you haven't caught my cold."

"No, Mother," Pauline said, "I haven't caught your *flu*. I've just had a disappointing day, making myself look silly in front of Inspector Peacock and Constable Wilson. I'm just angry with myself."

"I'm sure Inspector Peacock doesn't think you're silly."

"Maybe not but the word of this fiasco will be all around the local police by now and it will influence how they regard me in future. It's infuriating. I was so sure, too sure, and now I have to start all over again."

"What happened to cause all this?" her father asked.

"I'm not about to recount my folly to an even wider audience, thank you very much" Pauline said. "I'm going to bed." She stalked off up the stairs leaving her bemused parents watching her go.

# 16

# A GLIMMER OF HOPE – JANUARY 3

TRUE TO HER WORD, on January 3$^{rd}$, the first fine day since she'd last spoken to him, Pauline phoned Ramsay to confirm he was at work. Finding he was and willing to help, she drove up to Newcastle early in the morning with John Ogilvie and the will. The cold, clear weather meant the roads were dry and swept but it was still icy and slow-going in places, which meant it was almost lunchtime when she was ushered into Ramsay's office.

"Chief Inspector, this is John Ogilvie. He's the solicitor whose office has had the safekeeping of the will. He is sure that this isn't the will that was signed and witnessed by his father all those years ago."

The two men shook hands and Ramsay took the envelope, opened it, and drew out the disputed documents.

"They look the same, Miss Riddell. What are you hoping to achieve by having them microscopically examined?"

"The local police had the pages and ink checked, as I was telling you on the phone, and they say the ink and paper is the same for all three pages, which in their mind, means the will is genuine. Mr. Ogilvie can provide more details about that if your people need them. I thought more sophisticated equipment might be able to prove the three pages were not created at the same time."

"We'll go to the lab and find out, shall we?" Ramsay asked, picking up the phone and calling through to the lab. It took a moment or two of persuasion, but he finally hung up and signaled them to follow.

They followed him through the winding corridors of the old building into a block added on behind the station.

"I've never been to this new lab," Pauline said, as they put on coats, gloves, head coverings, and bootees over their shoes.

"I wish I didn't have to," Ramsay growled. "The new head of the department is a stickler for all this nonsense. I liked it when I could walk in smoking a pipe, covered in dirt from the crime scene, and with a group of partygoers in the last conscious state of drunkenness."

As Ramsay didn't actually smoke a pipe or anything at all, Pauline rightly surmised that the Chief Inspector was not in favor of modern lab codes.

Ramsay explained his purpose to the lab technician who approached to determine their presence was sanctioned. Finding it was, he pointed them to a small seating area for staff, took the will and hurried away to begin work.

"I don't like having the will out of my sight," Ogilvie said, refusing the seat Ramsay offered. "I won't be able to see it if I sit down."

After an hour, when they'd exhausted all the topics of conversation they had, mainly the weather and how peculiar this winter was, Ogilvie saw the technician hurrying to the director's office. His manner suggested something beyond confirmation of authenticity and they were all in varying states of excitement by the time the director himself approached, with the technician in tow.

"We might have something for you," the director said.

"We concur with the earlier investigation you mentioned, in that the paper and ink are of the same era on all three sheets of paper. However, where we think, and we'd need to have further tests done to be sure, we see a difference is in the ink and the aging of the paper."

"What does that mean?" Ramsay asked.

"First, the ink. It is the same age on all three sheets but the ink on the first sheet came from a different typewriter ribbon than the ink on the other two."

"That could mean the writer had to change ribbons after the first sheet, couldn't it?" Ogilvie asked.

"It could but the ink has aged differently to the other two sheets. We can't be certain, we'd have to do some tests to confirm, but we think the ink on sheet one was aged on the ribbon in its packaging while the ink on pages two and three aged on the paper, albeit in an envelope and in a dark place."

"So that's the typewriter..." Pauline began.

"Not quite," the technician said. "I think the wear on the keys is different between the first and other two pages."

"Are you saying there's more? As if it had been typed by the same machine but years later?" Ogilvie asked.

"Not exactly. There are no damaged keys and the font style is the same so in that sense it could be the same machine and it's not like in detective novels where there's a damaged letter. This is subtler than that. I think it's two different machines. The letters have worn differently and, if anything, the first page was typed on a newer machine."

"We did buy a replacement typewriter," Ogilvie said, thoughtfully. "It's some years ago. I'd have to check when."

"And the paper?" Pauline asked, her hopes rising with everything she heard.

"The same idea, really. They're the same age and from the same company, that much is true, but the aging is different. We think this first sheet was in a pack in a cupboard until fairly recently and the other two have aged together in a different location. Again, I repeat, we'd need to do proper aging tests to confirm this before we'd be prepared to go to court with our findings."

"How long would that take?" Ogilvie asked.

"It's hard to say but not less than six months to be relatively sure we were correct in our diagnosis."

"Six months!" Ogilvie cried.

"I'm afraid so. Can you get a court order to hold the reading of the will?"

"I shall have to," Ogilvie said, "but it will be challenged. And we still don't have the original will so the brothers may have to share the estate. It's not ideal. Still, I do thank you for giving us hope, Director. We have a path on which to make progress."

"I think I should say, however," the director said, "we are unlikely to be able to do the test. We're a police lab and don't do private work."

"Then what would you suggest?"

"Durham University, I know, has a machine and they do work for money. Failing that, York will have one, I'm sure, for the Jorvik excavations. You'll have heard of them, I expect. They found the old Viking city under the medieval and modern cities and they turned up many artefacts that needed aging. You could try them."

They had a late lunch with Ramsay before setting off, hoping to be back in Goathland before the light went, which would be around 3:30 at this time of the year. As they prepared to leave, and on being pressed to help, Ramsay said, "Nothing about this is in my area, Miss Riddell. However, if you have Inspector Peacock phone me, I will confirm to him everything we heard from the lab today."

With that, Pauline had to be satisfied, and thank him for the help he had given.

In the car, Pauline said, "I hope when you do wills these days, you have the owner and witnesses sign each sheet."

"I don't because we haven't in the past dealt with the kind of people who would make that kind of thing necessary," Ogilvie said. "We have, however, one of those photocopy machines and we place a signed copy of the original in a secondary but equally safe place."

"That's good," Pauline said, "but consider having all the will's pages signed or at least initialed too. It's easily done at the time of the will signing."

Ogilvie thought for a time and then said, "All our clients live in the local area and come into the village every week for something. I shall have them pop into the office and re-sign their wills."

"Please don't tell them it's because of the Thornton will."

"Certainly not," Ogilvie looked aghast at the mention of such indiscreet behavior. "If they ask, I'll say it's new advice from the Law Society, or some such thing."


"DID you get good news when you met your Chief Inspector?" Mrs. Riddell asked, as they were settling down for the night in front of the living room hearth. "After yesterday evening's gloom, tonight you look like the cat that got the cream."

"I got some hope, yes," Pauline said, and she recounted what had been suggested by the lab staff.

"That is good news," her father said. "A lot of people will be pleased to hear it."

Pauline was horrified. "They can't hear it," she said. "Not until there's sufficient evidence to back it up and that is months away."

"But Pauline," her mother said. "People on the Thornton estate are worried sick. It's like a huge weight hovering over their heads that can come down on them at any time. They have to be told."

"No!" Pauline snapped. "And if you want me to share anything with you in future you won't talk like this again. To raise their hopes only to have them crushed later is monstrous."

Taken aback by her daughter's vehemence, Mrs. Riddell asked, "But why would their hopes be dashed?"

Pauline explained about the estate being shared if the original will couldn't be found, and ended with, "Worse, the aging tests may not even prove it a forgery. We don't know. It just gives me enough hope to carry on. I'm sure it does very little for Frank Thornton."

"The original page will have been destroyed, surely," her father said. "Why would the forger keep it?"

Wary now of her parents' ability to keep secrets that they had no part in, Pauline said, "It probably has been destroyed but the best solution to this whole mess would be it being found."

"And you think Harry Clark was responsible for the forgery?" her father asked.

"He is the one who had the best opportunity," Pauline said, still wary. "After all, he typed up the original and he was in the office every day after. He had the keys to the safe and access to the supplies. But," she said firmly, "opportunity isn't proof. After all, old Mr. Ogilvie had access and so did the two clerks who've worked there since Harry retired."

Her mother shook her head. "No, I don't believe it" she said. "Harry Clark was the nicest, most timid man you'd ever meet. Even if he had wanted to do it, his conscience wouldn't have let him. Why, he lived in constant fear of his sister's sharp tongue, never mind the law."

"I didn't know he had a sister," Pauline said.

"After their parents died," Mr. Riddell said, "Harry and

his sister lived on in their parents' house. His sister died many years ago; she's buried in the churchyard near her parents' grave."

"Harry always said he wanted to be buried there too but sadly they never found his body," her mother added.

"Well, remember what I told you," Pauline said, rising to go up to her room, "nothing I share with you is to go outside these walls."

"We can hardly get out and go anywhere to tell anyone anyway, can we?" her father said.

"Not even over the phone," Pauline added. "Not a word. Whatever thoughts I have about people are just that, thoughts. I have no answers and certainly no proof. Don't let me down on this."

She received a sheepish sort of assent that did little to calm her nerves, but it was all she could hope for. *Again*, she thought, mentally chiding herself, *I've told people too much. I must learn to say less.*

# 17

# ANOTHER POSSIBLE SOLUTION –
## JANUARY 4

BY MORNING, her nerves had been restored by sleep and further soothed by the collecting and washing of the apparently inexhaustible supply of eggs the farm's hens produced. With the farm work done, she drove into the village, picked up John Ogilvie and they lost no time in calling on Frank Thornton to tell him what they'd learned from the lab.

"Then I shall call Durham and York to see who could do this kind of testing," Thornton said. "But it doesn't get us out of the difficulty around having this will read. What's your advice, John?"

"The difficulty, as I see it, is the bequests to your staff, your father's staff as was. Some of them are very old and could die before the will is proven. I think we have to at least make that part public and maybe announce the challenge to the main bequests."

"Can we do that?" Thornton asked.

"I need to confirm but maybe, if you could see your way to paying those bequests without publicizing the will, it would be better," the lawyer said.

"Meanwhile, John," Thornton said, "you and I should find an organization that can prove this will is a forgery. I must thank you again for that, Miss Riddell. Your assistance there has been invaluable."

"You still have the problem of what happens when the will is invalidated," Pauline said. "You and your brother would share equally, under the law."

"That's better than the present case, though," Thornton said, "where I get only five hundred pounds. In the case of being without the will, I could take out a mortgage and buy out my brother. He might go for that, if it meant money immediately rather than a long, drawn out negotiation with developers."

"I fear it may come to that, though your brother will demand a high price you can be sure," Pauline said. "However, I did wonder if good old Harry mightn't have kept the first page as insurance."

"If he did, it would have gone with him to his house in Spain," Thornton said, almost thinking aloud. "He'd want it close at hand, I think. I understand the house is being sold. He left it to a second cousin, who doesn't like going to Spain apparently and has put it up for sale."

"I wonder if we could have it searched before it is gone?" Pauline asked.

"I hear it has been broken into on more than one occasion," Ogilvie added, "which is part of the reason the owner is trying to sell."

"That makes me even more convinced the first page was kept," Pauline said. "The question is, did he get it?"

"Who?" Frank Thornton said.

"Your brother," Pauline replied, trying to keep the exasperation out of her voice.

"You think he's a burglar as well as a swindler, forger, gambler, and womanizer?"

"I suspect he might be, yes."

"I've had a thought," Ogilvie interjected, in case

Thornton family solidarity overcame Frank's fears. "Old Harry's lawyer is in Whitby. I should ask if any papers or things of that sort were handed over to Harry's cousin by the will. It's possible Harry didn't keep the first page with him so it couldn't be forced from him if they came after him."

"Lawyer to lawyer is the way to start that conversation," Pauline agreed. "Then we need to speak to good old Harry's cousin. Is he an honest man?"

"I believe so," Thornton said, "but then we all thought Harry was too."

"If we speak to him, we mustn't raise his suspicions. He may not know what he has. If he finds out, he may want a price to part with it," Pauline said.

"You have a horribly cynical view of people, Miss Riddell," Ogilvie said. "The man is a churchwarden, a businessman, and very respectable."

Pauline laughed. "A businessman and a churchwarden," she said. "Then expect to haggle."

# 18

# BACK TO THE FRENCH PAINTER –
# JANUARY 5

THE WEATHER REMAINED cold but more snow had drifted across the track from the farm to the lane, though the road along the dale was clear again. Her father flattened down the snow from the farm to the road leaving deep, icy ruts where the tractors wheels had sunk in. Pauline was able to make her way to the outside world but only by using her parent's old Land Rover. Her own car would never make it to the lane.

Pauline drove into Goathland, intending to catch Mrs. Drayton before or after church. As she passed John Ogilvie's office, she saw lights on and stopped. Inside the office, she could see the lawyer moving about. She locked her car and rang the office bell.

Ogilvie opened the door and greeted her like a long-lost friend. "Miss Riddell, this is a pleasant surprise. To what do I owe the pleasure?"

"I was passing, saw you in the office and thought I'd pop in to see if you'd heard any more about Harry's will?"

"I haven't been able to speak to the cousin yet. There's still no answer when I call."

"These holidays," Pauline said in exasperation, "or maybe it's the weather. We're blocked every step of the way."

"And you?"

"I'm off to ask Mrs. Drayton for more information about the Frenchwoman. I hope to catch her at church."

"I don't think Mrs. Drayton is a churchgoer," he said. "I usually see her in the shop on Sunday morning. Doing stock keeping or the books, I imagine."

"I had her down as a chapel sort of person," Pauline said. "But I'll try the post office first, thank you."

"I had better be going as well," Ogilvie said. "My wife will never forgive me if I'm late for the morning service. I wish you luck with Mrs. Drayton. She's one of those witnesses who will tell you everything about everybody until the moment you ask them to speak to someone in authority and then she knows nothing."

Pauline laughed. "I know that type," she said, "and I feel I'd do much better if I were more local, but I must try to win her over. The name of the Frenchwoman would be a start."

"You know, even I saw this mysterious woman occasionally but never close enough to speak to."

"What did you think?"

"She was a bit of an odd figure, slim and angular. There was none of that womanliness we associate with the French. She was probably attractive enough as a young woman, I expect, but adversity has a way of making its mark on us all."

Pauline nodded. "All our lives have been marked, it's true, and she will have lived through an even more horrible time in the drawn-out North African wars."

She took her leave of Ogilvie and quickly crossed the street to the post office where she found Mrs. Drayton dusting and re-arranging the shop's small stock of goods.

"A slow day, Mrs. Drayton," Pauline said, as she closed the door behind her.

The postmistress's face brightened immediately. "Good morning," she said. "They've all been slow days since we had that snow on Christmas Eve, but I'm not actually open on Sunday."

"And I'm not a big spender either, I'm afraid," Pauline said. "I just want a book of stamps. I like to reply to my Christmas card senders quickly, before I forget. I won't know all of them until I get home, of course, but I brought with me those I'd received when I came away. My mother was ill, you see, and I came to help out."

"I'm sure your parents were pleased," the postmistress said, opening a drawer behind the counter where the stamp books were kept.

Pauline smiled, remembering her mother's crossly worded retort that she needed no help from anyone and neither did her husband.

"I'm sure they are," Pauline said. "Forgive my curiosity but do you remember the full name of that French artist that stayed at the Dower house?"

"I didn't take much notice," the postmistress said.

This was a statement Pauline could not believe. A foreigner staying in the village, the whole village would be agog with excitement, and Mrs. Drayton the only one who would know.

"Please try," Pauline said. "It might be important."

"Who to?"

"To anyone trying to make sense of what's been going on here," Pauline said.

"I heard you'd been asked to snoop and pry."

"Then you were misinformed, Mrs. Drayton," Pauline said gently. "I think people have misunderstood. I asked Constable Wilson about the events and when we finished speaking, I told him I'd share with him anything I heard. I'm not investigating, only interested."

"If Constable Wilson wants to know, he can ask me."

"I'll certainly suggest that to him," Pauline said. "Now, how much do I owe you for those stamps?"

Sensing she was upsetting a potentially lucrative customer, the postmistress said, "It was Nicole and something like Dubois."

She pronounced it Dooboys, which Pauline couldn't translate into a possible name but she thanked the woman and left the shop. Her next stop in the village had to be the police house where she hoped to have a better idea of the name than Mrs. Drayton had managed. At the Police House, she was welcomed in like a long-lost friend, which was gratifying. She'd half expected Constable Wilson would still be angry over the Dower house fiasco but he ushered her into his office and pulled up a seat for her with old-fashioned gallantry.

"Good day, Miss Riddell," Wilson said when she was seated. "To what do I owe this pleasure?"

"I want to know who the Frenchwoman was," Pauline said, "and I hoped by now you may know."

"I do. When I started looking into the incidents, she was still at the Dower house," Wilson said. "Since we last spoke, I've talked to the French authorities and delved into her background. Her name is Nicole Dubois and she lives in a small village near St. Tropez, which is how she came to know Anthony Thornton, of course."

"I wondered if she might be more than just an acquaintance of Thornton's," Pauline said. "I wondered if she might be his wife."

"Not according to the French police, Miss Riddell," Wilson said. "They say she lives nearby."

"It's infuriating," Pauline said. "I'm sure these events are all connected but everything that should link them doesn't."

"Maybe because they're not. I'm not a famous detective

like you, Miss Riddell, but it seems to me it's only in books everything ties neatly together in life."

Pauline laughed. "Of course, you're right," she said. "Real life isn't neat but the timing of these is too tight to be coincidental."

"The will was forged years ago," Wilson reminded her. "It isn't recent like the murder and the robberies and other than your cousin Walter being a bit of a rogue, there's no reason to think even they are linked."

"I know, I know," Pauline said, "but I still feel I'm right."

"It's evidence that determines the outcome, not feelings – as I'm sure you know," Wilson said.

"But it's feelings that drive our desire for evidence," Pauline said. "And even you admit to having hunches."

"True, some things you just know are right but I don't feel it in this case."

"And right now, the information you've just given me seems to suggest your hunch is right and mine wrong," Pauline said, laughing, "but I won't give up just yet."

Although she'd laughed off her puzzlement to Constable Wilson, as she walked back to her car her spirits were once again gloomy. All her theories seemed to be draining away to nothingness.

# 19

# THE BROTHER ARRIVES - JANUARY 6

NEXT MORNING, Pauline had only just finished her morning chores when the phone rang. It was Frank Thornton.

"Good morning, Miss Riddell," he began, "I hoped I'd catch you before you set out on the trail of our wrongdoers."

"I'm not sure I have an active trail to follow right now," Pauline said. "Until we hear back from someone, there's not a lot to chase."

"Well, I've heard from someone," he said. Pauline could hear the grim humor in his voice.

"Your brother?" she asked.

"Exactly. My dear brother has phoned to say he's catching a train and I'm to have him picked up at York Station. Our surmising was correct. He wants to know why the will isn't being read."

"Did he say that?"

Frank laughed. "He thinks he's too clever by half so no he didn't say that. He just wants to see me and the old place."

"He isn't planning to stay in his own house, then."

"Too much expense, I'd guess," Thornton replied. "Anyway, I thought you might want to meet him. A social call, of course."

"Perhaps you should invite some other neighbors too. That way I don't stand out quite so much."

"I don't imagine he will have heard of you, Miss Riddell, but I take your point. I'll invite some neighbors including you and your parents."

"We will be happy to accept," Pauline said. "I look forward to meeting your brother."

* * *

PAULINE and her parents were sitting down to lunch when the phone rang. It was Frank Thornton again.

After the usual greetings, he said, "I have some good news. The people at the Viking dig in York will be happy to accept the challenge of identifying the age of the will's sheets of paper and earning some money in the process. It seems their costs generally exceed their grants and they welcome donations of all kinds."

"I imagine they do," Pauline said. "Asking Yorkshire folk to hand over cash for studying ancient remains will always be a challenge. It's not by chance the Yorkshireman's motto is the 'Four Alls'."

Frank laughed. "Hear all, see all, say nought. Eat all, drink all, pay nought. And if you do ought for nought, you do it for yourself. It's a good motto to live by, even if I, as a Yorkshireman, do say so."

"And I, as a Yorkshire woman, second it a little but it can be wearisome sometimes," Pauline answered, thinking of the many improvements she'd like to make around her parents' house.

"They can't give me an expected finish date until they've seen the will."

"The longer it lasts, the more it will cost," Pauline replied.

"I'd be sure they give you a clear plan, schedule and price before letting them loose."

"I will. I'm getting used to dealing with contractors," Thornton said, "now my estate manager is retired."

"I presume your brother isn't aware of any of this?"

"That's right and that reminds me of the other reason I called. He came back from the pub last night in a surly mood. Someone had told him there was a nosy woman sniffing around the village and investigating the strange things that have been happening."

"That's disappointing," Pauline said. "Does he know who the nosy woman is?"

"I don't think so but I'm sure another night at the pub and he'll know everything about you. He will soon put two and two together and realize you could also be looking into the will."

"Nobody in the pub should know that," Pauline said.

"I suspect his own guilty conscience will make the connection for him."

Pauline considered. "We'll wait until he and I meet at your soiree tomorrow. If it's clear he does suspect, we'll have to have a different plan."

"Plan?"

"Yes," Pauline said. "My plan right now is to meet him and attempt to catch him out, linking the incidents and the will to the murder, which will give us enough to bring Inspector Peacock into it."

"How do you intend to manage that?"

"I haven't got that far in my plan, but I still have a day to think of it," Pauline said. "Otherwise, something more direct must be employed."

# 20

# THORNTON MANOR SOIREE –
# JANUARY 7

THE FOLLOWING EVENING, Pauline and her parents were ushered into the manor's large entertaining room and welcomed by the host and a small party of their neighbors.

"Miss Riddell," Frank Thornton said, approaching with a flamboyantly dressed man in tow. "I think you're probably the only person here who's never met my brother. Anthony, this is Pauline Riddell, you'll remember her parents of course. Miss Riddell, my brother Anthony."

He took her proffered hand in a firm grip that belied the dissolute appearance of the rest of him. The newspaper photo had flattered him for, though younger than his brother, in the actual flesh he looked ten years older.

"You live in the south of France, I believe," Pauline said.

"I do. Love the heat. Can't stand the cold. Coming here reminds me why I live there," he said tersely.

"I love all the seasons," Pauline said, "but after the past week or so, I can appreciate your point of view much better."

He nodded and, without another word, left to refill his glass. Frank hadn't brought in extra staff to wait on his guests, Pauline noticed. She wondered if that was to remind Anthony how parlous the situation was and how hard Frank would be hit if the forged will stood. If it was, she doubted such considerations would weigh on his brother's conscience.

Anthony may not have been taken with *her*, she noticed wryly, but he quickly descended on the corner where three young people, two girls and a boy, were holding themselves aloof from the old people. Pauline could see that however dismissive he was with people of his own age, he did have a way with young women and they were soon giggling at his stories and eager to hear more. The young man was clearly put in the shade.

"Well, Miss Riddell, what do you think of my brother?"

Pauline had been so engrossed in watching his brother, she'd missed Frank's approach and she was startled by the question.

"I have very little to go on," she said, smiling. "He took one look at me and fled."

"Unfortunately, he'd heard of you," Thornton said. "Not from me, you should know, but someone told him."

"Do you think it was before he came or only since he arrived?"

"He's spent time in the pub both nights," Thornton said. "I guess it was there. How would he know otherwise?"

"I'm suspicious of everything," Pauline said, smiling. "Still, I'm sorry he learned of my involvement. I'd hoped to have a normal conversation with him before he found out."

"Do you think he'd have said anything incriminating?"

Pauline laughed. "I'm sure he's very good at playing his cards close to his chest but I hoped he'd say something unwise because he didn't know what I know. People who like to talk and spin entertaining tales often do. Does he ever talk about his wife?"

Thornton shook his head. "He says she doesn't like to travel if I ask. It's possible they separated years ago. That's how little I know about her."

"His wife doesn't seem to be on his mind right now," Pauline said, gesturing to the corner where Anthony had practically cornered the two young women, leaving the young man isolated.

"My brother likes to socialize," Frank said, shortly. "He always did."

"I think there may be two fathers in the room that will be collecting their daughters in a short time," Pauline suggested, smiling.

"Anthony likes to flirt with pretty young women but they're quite safe. No harm will befall *them*."

Unsure she'd understood him rightly, Pauline was about to ask what he meant but people approached them so she turned to a less sensitive topic. "Have you explained about the will?"

"I did today," Thornton said.

"How did your brother take that news?"

"Not well, as you can imagine. He's visiting a lawyer tomorrow to see what can be done about my refusal to have the will proceed at once. He says if I don't want it read, it must be because it gives him more money than was expected and he needs that money."

"What does John Ogilvie say about when a will must be read?" Pauline asked.

"There's no explicit time for a will to be read and, anyway, the beneficiaries can't get paid until all taxes and debts have been settled. Obviously, all this has to be done in a reasonable time because inheritance tax must be paid within six months. However, with such a straightforward will, John feels waiting months for the test might be considered extreme by any judge, particularly as the will has been examined by Police and declared not to be a forgery."

"Six months is perfect," Pauline said, happy to hear some good news. "The test results will almost certainly be back by then. Just say the will must wait until then. Let your brother get his lawyer and have Ogilvie stall them."

"That's the position we will have to take for now, but my brother is angry, desperate, even."

"Your brother can try to get some legal backing and have the swift winding up of your father's estate," Pauline said, "but lawyers cost money. They don't work for free. If he has as little as he claims, you may be safe."

Thornton nodded. "I hope so, but I fear not," he said. "He seems truly desperate. I wish we hadn't had the local police lab examine the will. We've handed Tony the ammunition he needs to win his case if he discovers that."

"But he doesn't know, does he?"

"I hope not or we really are done for. We must be sure he never finds out."

"There's only a small number of people who know about the examination," Pauline said. "We must make sure they don't talk."

"What if they've already talked?"

"I haven't heard anyone gossiping about it," Pauline said.

"With all due respect, Miss Riddell, few people around this neighborhood are likely to take you into their confidence, are they?"

Pauline grimaced. That was true. "But neither Alan nor my parents have mentioned any whispers about it, so I have some confidence."

"Tony would promise to pay a lot of money for information that would help him," Thornton said, "and you can be sure he's putting feelers out."

"I'll warn my family," Pauline said. "You must warn John Ogilvie. His clerk may know and see a risk-free opportunity."

"Without the information about the police examination, he may struggle to get a lawyer to take action right now. The short time, the bad weather and the flu would all be considered mitigating factors by a judge, I would think."

Pauline nodded. "For now, yes, but if your brother is desperate, he'll push to get action started." She paused, "Do you know if he does really need cash right now? Or is it just he hopes at last for the completion of a long-planned scheme?"

Thornton considered. "You know, I do think he's desperate. He's never visited me before, even when he came to stay at his house. But it must be something recent. There was no sense of it in that infamous letter he sent."

"Why doesn't he sell the Dower house?"

"He can't. It's left to him for his lifetime and then it reverts to the estate. I think my father hoped he'd live there, settle and become an upright citizen when he matured."

"I wonder if he's lost a lot of money to some unpleasant types, the kind of people we read about in the more lurid papers?"

"You think the Kray twins are after him?" Thornton said, grinning. The Kray twins were a couple of particularly unpleasant London gangsters whose doings were always in the newspapers.

"Not necessarily them but someone like them. They can't be the only mobsters down there in London."

"And he came here when their attentions became too marked?"

"Exactly, before he got too marked himself."

Thornton laughed. "I'll ask him, but he won't tell me," he said.

"But Inspector Peacock may be able to find out," Pauline said thoughtfully. "After all, if there's someone escaping London mobsters on his patch, he'll want to know about it. I'll phone him and see what he can do."

. . .

INSPECTOR PEACOCK AGREED he did want to know of possible future bodily harm to someone in his jurisdiction when, after she returned home, Pauline called and put him in possession of her suspicions and Frank Thornton's view it might well be so.

"I'm getting to speak to my colleagues in the London police more often since you arrived, Miss Riddell. I don't know whether to be pleased about that or not."

"It may prove to be a good career move, Inspector, particularly if this case, when it becomes public knowledge, attracts press attention."

"Provided the case ends satisfactorily, it might," he said. "At this moment, I'm not seeing a satisfying end to my murder investigation, you seem to be floundering on the will, and Constable Wilson is no further forward on the ugly incidents and robberies."

"I think the will question is already solved, we just need time to prove it, and the incidents and murder, I'm sure, will prove to be part of that. When any one of the three is solved, they all will be."

"Apart from your intuition, Miss Riddell, there's nothing actually to connect them at all yet."

"Intuition is your subconscious mind making connections your conscious mind hasn't yet seen," Pauline said firmly.

"So they say," Peacock replied, "but the justice branch of the state requires some proof. Until we have that, they're separate."

"On a slightly different topic, Inspector," Pauline said, quietly. "Can you and I talk somewhere privately tomorrow?"

"I was returning to the crime scene tomorrow for a final viewing before we release it," Peacock said. "We could meet there, if you wish."

# 21

# A SECOND SETBACK – JANUARY 8

PAULINE PARKED her car in the yard at Walter's cottage, alongside the police car where a bored looking driver sat inside, tapping his fingers on the steering wheel. She nodded to the police guard on the door, who told her to go inside where the inspector was expecting her.

"Ah, Miss Riddell," Peacock said as he saw her entering the small hallway. "I thought I heard a car."

Pauline looked about. "Are we alone?" she asked.

He nodded. "Yes. This is very mysterious."

"Not really," Pauline said. "It's just I want to talk of things that are somewhat sensitive, and I don't want word of it to get out to my many relations in the neighborhood."

Peacock laughed. "I can see this must be a difficult case for you. We usually re-assign someone who has close connections to people involved with a crime. You, however, can't do that."

"Worse. My family expect me to do something but get angry if I suggest something they don't like or ask a question they think reflects badly on them."

"What's today's issue?"

"I'm sure you're aware my cousin dabbled in smuggling,"

she said. "I wondered if you'd had any sense his death came from that, rather than poaching, say."

"I had heard that, and I do think it far more likely the quarrel came from smuggling than poaching. I've never heard of poachers being bumped off over a few rabbits or pheasants."

"I imagine it happens," Pauline said, "but, in general, I agree with you. My question is who were Walter's contacts in that world? Do you know?"

"You are supposed to be investigating a forged will and helping Constable Wilson with some ugly incidents, Miss Riddell," Peacock said, "not concerning yourself with murder."

Pauline had anticipated this response. "And, as I've said before, Inspector, these crimes are linked. I don't yet know how but knowing who Walter's confederates were may help identify the burglaries."

"Hmm," Peacock said, "stretching it a bit but I'll go along with it this time. On the shipping side, we have no idea. He doesn't seem to have taken anyone into his confidence as to the boats and the captains he dealt with."

"That doesn't surprise me," Pauline said, "but it's annoying."

"It hardly matters," Peacock said. "They may be defrauding Customs and Excise, but the boats are fishing trawlers not ocean liners. Their carrying capacity is tiny and your cousin couldn't have carried much away with him even if they did."

"He bought that new van recently," Pauline reminded him. "That suggests scaling up the business."

"Perhaps, but there's no sign of illicit cargo here and no one saw him at the local harbors recently so I don't think the trouble came from the shipping side of the smuggling."

"And on the distribution side?"

"That's where it does get more interesting," Peacock said. "People have seen one or possibly two well-dressed men talking to your cousin in the weeks before his death."

"Two sightings of well-dressed men or more?"

"Possibly more. People don't remember the dates and times very well and the descriptions are vague. The witnesses only noticed the clothes really."

"When they say, well-dressed," Pauline asked, "do they mean expensive clothes or gentlemanly clothes?"

"Your guess is as good as mine," Peacock said. "I'm not sure they'd know the difference, would they?"

"The witnesses didn't say flashy, like a gangster, for instance?"

Peacock thought. "No," he said. "I think you're probably right. It wasn't some tasteless mobster. These are country folk. They don't like that kind of fashion and wouldn't call it well-dressed."

"But they didn't recognize the men so at least it isn't some local landowner trying to keep his impoverished estate together."

"If you're thinking of Mr. Thornton, you're wrong. They didn't recognize the man or men."

"I wasn't thinking of Mr. Thornton," Pauline said, "but he isn't the only gentleman in the country whose home and lands are struggling. They pretty well all are."

"You sound as if you speak from experience," Peacock said.

"There's a local family near where I live, who have chopped down every tree on their estate to pay off death duties and hang on to what is their own land. What was a beautiful park a year ago looks like a lunar landscape now."

Peacock nodded. "True enough," he said, "we have some around here in the same predicament, though I think they're just selling up rather than fighting to stay. Maybe we should be looking closer to home for our distributor. We were thinking Leeds or Manchester as the likely home of your cousin's mysterious visitors."

"Have you any clear idea what sort of goods were being smuggled?" Pauline asked. While she had Peacock in an expansive mood it seemed like a good idea to continue.

"Like I said, there's no evidence here to show what, but I imagine it was the usual: tobacco and alcohol. If we had a big drug problem, I'd think maybe heroin, but we don't."

"I'm pleased to hear it," she said. "I'd hate something like that to become known. My family are old-fashioned about things like drugs. From what you say, Inspector, this doesn't sound like anything more than my family suspected: bottles of brandy and cartons of cigarettes. Is that a fair assessment?"

Peacock nodded. "I'd say so. Hardly more than the well-to-do vacationer who takes his car to the continents smuggles. Now let me ask you a question. Have you any new information that links the murder with the will and the burglaries?"

"The will maybe not, but the burglars needed someone to sell on the goods. It occurred to me Walter may have become involved in that way and there was a falling out among thieves."

"I see, but that means if it isn't related to the will, the three crimes are not all linked."

Pauline laughed. "I may believe something to be true, Inspector, but that doesn't mean I don't look at other possibilities and this is another possibility."

"Very wise, Miss Riddell. Now, if there's nothing else you want to know, I'll return to this last viewing of the crime scene. Your extended family want the cottage released for sale."

"Nothing else, Inspector," Pauline said and left him to his solitary examination. She had another important meeting to attend, though it probably wouldn't look that way to Inspector Peacock. He'd think it was just socializing.

* * *

FRANK THORNTON, once launched on the career of amiable host by Pauline, was really blossoming. A second soiree at Thornton Manor was unheard of in recent memory. The neighbors, however, seemed to welcome the new social life beginning to emerge from the manor house. With old Mr. Thornton ill for so long, there'd been a gap in the entertainment calendar that Frank showed signs of filling.

Pauline however, had a more serious motive for encouraging and supporting these evening events. First, it kept Anthony Thornton from brooding and plotting in pubs for one night of the week at least, and secondly, it meant she could engage with him without him having an easy means of escape. It was possible he was innocent of all the things she suspected but she thought not.

Anthony Thornton became detached from a group of neighbors for a moment, and Pauline pounced. "Mr. Thornton," she said, "it's nice to see you again. I hear you've been busy."

His expression was bland though she could sense his anger; his reply was calm enough. "Busy?" he asked, continuing to walk to the drinks table with Pauline doggedly alongside.

"Looking for a lawyer to speed up the reading of the will."

"And why shouldn't I?"

"No reason," Pauline said. "I just wondered why you would do that." At this stage, she felt there was nothing to be lost by openly stating her interest in the progress of the will.

"Because," he said, "and I've already told my brother

this, I knew something he clearly didn't. I'm sorry our father was so secretive on the subject, but it can't be helped. The will was changed by our father some years ago."

"Why?"

"Because he came to believe, as I do, the future is more important than the past."

"Can you explain what you mean by that?"

"No, Miss Riddell, I won't," he said. "My brother can explain it. I told him this afternoon and you can see by how sick he looks that he is beginning to believe what I said."

He walked quickly away, leaving Pauline to observe Frank Thornton as he mingled with his guests. Anthony was right about Frank's expression, he looked like a man going to the scaffold.

When she saw him break away from one knot of neighbors, Pauline crossed the floor quickly and caught him before he could start talking to another.

"Mr. Thornton," she said. "I think you're avoiding me."

He laughed but there was no humor in it. "Not at all, Miss Riddell," he said. "I have had some news and I've been trying to work out how to tell you. I think I may have set you investigating something that has a simple, rational explanation after all."

"Then please explain," Pauline said, "because your brother hinted as much and I'm at a loss to understand how this can be explained away innocently."

He quickly outlined the story his brother had told him. How his father had come to believe Anthony's plans for the estate, far from being ugly and abhorrent, were actually good because they represented a growing future, while Frank's plans were a slow death for everyone.

"Is this likely though, Mr. Thornton?" Pauline asked. "Was your father the kind of man who would change so dramatically?"

"He was very ill and irritable these past years. The pain was often intense, and I can almost believe he would, seeing his own death nearing, believe the estate should die too."

"Very Wagnerian," Pauline said. "Do you have a lot of Viking blood in your line? Have the Thorntons down the centuries immolated themselves to celebrate their passing? I think it sounds like what it is, Mr. Thornton. A story. Admittedly, a clever one, but a story nonetheless."

"I'd like to agree, Miss Riddell, but there's no way of proving it and it checkmates our aging tests of the forgery."

Pauline nodded. "I saw that too. Someone talked and this story is the result. It answers every objection and is completely unprovable, either way. A neutral judge would likely find in favor of your brother."

"I'm considering ending the aging tests," Frank Thornton said. "They won't help now. At least I'd save some money for my future."

"It's too soon for that," Pauline said, "and anyway, the money you saved would be Anthony's money if the law goes his way, not yours."

"You aren't cheering me up, Miss Riddell, and isn't that what guests at a soiree are expected to do?"

"I'm not feeling very happy myself, Mr. Thornton," Pauline said. "It seemed to me we had a clear path to overturning your brother's scheme and he's completely outfoxed us."

"As you say, Miss Riddell, we are further behind now than we were at the start."

"It always looks darkest before dawn," Pauline replied bracingly, but she didn't feel bracing. This was a serious setback.

"So they say," Thornton replied. "However, at this moment. I'm thinking I should just cut my losses. Unlike my brother, I'm not a gambling man and I have no taste for this kind of intrigue."

"You have nothing to lose by staying the course, Mr. Thornton. I'm sure you'll have good news very soon. Meanwhile do nothing," Pauline said.

# 22

# BACK TO THE WILL – JANUARY 9

"YOU AGAIN?" Sam Tunstall said in disgust. He was making his way over the snow-covered parking lot to the door of The Shepherds Arms unamused to find Pauline stepping in front of him.

Pauline smiled. "Yes, me again. I won't keep you long from your lunch," she said, moving to prevent him going around her.

"You are keeping me from my lunch," he said, which was true, of course.

"Can you tell me more about the well-dressed man you saw talking to Walter," Pauline asked.

"What more is there to tell? I seen them talking, along that lane that runs off the high road. They were quarter of a mile away, like, and the fella had his back to me."

"So, you wouldn't recognize him?"

"Nay, lass," Sam said. "He were too far and I only saw his back. I told you this afore."

"Do you know Anthony Thornton?"

"Him! I seen him when he were here a year or two back but know him, nay."

"Could it have been him?"

"It coulda bin anyone," Sam said exasperated.

"You said well-dressed," Pauline said. "Do you mean like a gentleman or a flashy sort of man?"

"He wore a tidy-looking brown coat, and brown trousers. His hat were a trilby and brown to match his coat. I couldn't tell if he was a gentleman but he wasn't, I think, a bookies-runner kind of character."

"I was thinking it may be someone who bought Walter's free trading goods," Pauline said, "particularly expensive goods like brandy or cigars."

"Aye, it coulda been," Sam agreed, "but I couldn't tell from what I saw."

"His build," Pauline persisted. "Was it familiar? Did he look like anyone you know? Someone from these parts?"

Sam shook his head. "Nothing about him reminded me of anyone. He just looked a well-to-do kind of man, whether from wealth or from work, I couldn't say."

Pauline frowned. She'd hoped for more than this. She'd hoped to find some detail Sam had missed in his earlier statement and, so far, that hadn't happened.

"What about his car? Could you see that?"

"Aye, it were a Morris Minor, blue," Sam said.

"I don't suppose you remember its number?"

Sam's expression made it clear he thought she'd lost her mind.

"Too far away," Pauline said.

He nodded. "Aye," he said, tersely.

"Did he look like a Morris Minor sort of driver?"

Sam seemed about to respond sharply but hesitated, then said, "Now you say that, it makes me think and what I think is he didn't look like someone who would have such a family kind of car."

"Can you think why that was?"

Sam shook his head. "Nay," he said, "he just looked like someone who normally rode in classier cars."

"Now you're thinking that way, does that bring anything else to mind?"

"I just seen them when I were passing the lane end," Sam said. "I didn't stop to inspect them so no, nothing else."

"All right, thank you, Sam," Pauline said. "I'll let you get to your ploughman's lunch."

Sam grimaced. "On a day like this, cold cheese and bread aren't appealing," he said. "A steak and kidney pudding is what I'm looking forward to."

Pauline walked back to her car in thought. Was Sam's 'a classier kind of car' idea enough to persuade Inspector Peacock to check again with the border authorities for Anthony Thornton's entering the country? She drove back to her parent's farm determined to call the moment she was home.

The police at Whitby station weren't inclined to say where the inspector was, only saying he'd gone to visit a crime scene. Frustrated, Pauline called Constable Wilson and was pleased to find her guess correct.

"Miss Riddell," Inspector Peacock said, when Constable Wilson handed him the phone. "Maybe you could join us here at the village police house. It's more secure, fewer people listening-in."

Pauline was annoyed at the suggestion her parents would overhear and spread what they heard but she couldn't deny it was possible and, as she was planning to ask for police investigations into the local bigwig's family, who just happened to be the owner of her parents' and brother's farms, she had to agree it made sense.

"I will be there in thirty minutes," she said, hanging up the phone.

It was a little more than that by the time Mrs. Wilson

ushered her into the police house and led her into the constable's office but it was close enough.

"The roads are still slippery," she said to DI Peacock by way of explanation, who was not looking at his watch, but Pauline couldn't help thinking he had been.

"They are," he agreed, "it's a peculiarly bad winter." He waited while Constable Wilson placed a chair at her disposal, and then continued, "take a seat, Miss Riddell, and we can discuss where we are on our investigations and what it was you were phoning me about."

"You start," Pauline said. "I need a minute to collect my thoughts. I had a rather nasty scare on the way over here and it will take me a moment to recover."

"Your car is all right?" Wilson asked.

"Yes, thank you. I didn't go off the road just slithered a bit. Nothing hurt, except my pride. You should understand I consider myself a very good driver, and these icy skids remind me no one is infallible."

"Then I suggest you start, Constable," Peacock said, "and I'll go next."

Constable Wilson reviewed the steps he'd taken to get to the bottom of the incidents and burglaries, including interviewing known fences and having the description of all the silver items circulated to jewelers and pawnshops throughout the county.

"Oh, it's to that matter, I was contacting you, Inspector," Pauline said, interjecting. "We know that Walter was seen talking to a well-dressed man and it occurred to me that might be Anthony Thornton. He said he wasn't in the country at the time. I wondered if you could ask our border people to confirm or deny that?"

"I could," Peacock said, "but it seems a long shot. A well-dressed man could be literally any one of a million men in the north of England. Why should we research someone who wouldn't have said he was in the country if he wasn't confident our research would prove exactly that?"

"As I understand it, if he came in from Ireland," Pauline said, "he wouldn't show up on our records. Can we ask the Irish police to check?"

"They would need some serious paperwork to hand over such information to us."

"I was afraid you'd say that," Pauline said before adding the information she'd been given by Sam. "So, you see," she added, "it's someone a bit above the ordinary for the folks around here."

"All right, I'll see what can be done," Peacock said. He turned to Constable Wilson and asked, "Did you get a sense any of the jewelers were suspect?"

Wilson shook his head. "I didn't," he said, "though some as we know wouldn't be above taking the loot and selling it on."

"And with a description as vague as the one you've given us, Miss Riddell," Peacock said. "That's not going to change. If we get some confirmation that Anthony Thornton did enter the country earlier than he said, we might have something to build on."

"Have you made progress on the murder, Inspector?" Pauline said. Her own views on that were coming more clearly into focus but she did want to know the police were eliminating all the alternatives.

"Not really," he admitted. "There's no evidence to go on. There are no fingerprints in the house that we haven't been able to account for and there was nothing on the body or clothes to point to any particular individual. I've no doubt it was a poaching or more likely a smuggling accomplice, though I can't see a reason why they should fall out this violently."

"You've interviewed his known associates?"

"Of course," Peacock said. "We haven't been idling our time away, even though it is the holiday season and the weather is awful. We've interviewed dozens of people and no one can explain this at all. The law may consider your cousin a bad man, but his neighbors don't. To a man, and woman, they're sorry he's dead and can't believe someone would do this."

"I think providing people with small luxuries for a reduced cost would make someone popular," Pauline said drily. "However, I also remember him as a charming man, so I know there's more to it than that."

"I knew your cousin quite well, Miss Riddell," Constable Wilson said, "and I'd agree with you. Even though I've often investigated crimes that I'm sure he committed, I liked him as a person and I'm sorry he's dead."

"To what would you attribute his likeability?" Peacock asked, somewhat bemused.

"His sense of humor," Pauline said. "He was always kidding. He used to tease me all the time, but he didn't mean anything by it."

"It's true," Wilson said. "Though some didn't see the humor sometimes."

"That's it?" Peacock said.

"No, of course not," Pauline said. "That was just what comes to mind. He was also kind, helpful, and went out of his way for those less fortunate than himself."

"Even that was misunderstood sometimes," Wilson said. "He stepped in to defend some newcomers to the district once and they took offence, not seeing him as a worthy champion, like."

Pauline laughed. "He did get into scrapes, even as a child, and that often got us into trouble too. And our parents didn't like being teased by a child any more than I'm sure other people did."

"He may have teased the wrong man this time," Peacock said.

Pauline nodded but said, "You don't kill people because they've made fun of you though, do you?"

"Perhaps not. Back to what I was saying, we have built a pretty clear picture of his final days but not his final hours. He left Whitby, where he'd been doing errands, and arrived home late in the afternoon, after dark, and that's the last we know of him until he turned up dead."

"Sometime between then – about four pm and eight o'clock when Sam Tunstall came to spend a convivial evening drinking with him – someone arrived at the house and killed him. Was the pathologist able to give a good time of death?"

Peacock grimaced. "You know experts," he said, "they give you a vague answer that they hedge around with disclaimers until there's nothing left in their words. He thinks five pm but mentions the cold out on the moor to say his estimate could vary by hours."

"The range being wider than the times you can pinpoint from the events?" Pauline asked, grinning.

Peacock nodded. "Got it in one, Miss Riddell. Anywhere from four to ten pm is our expert's pronouncement."

"Had he eaten?"

Peacock shook his head. "No, and he hadn't begun preparing an evening meal either, so I think the killer saw him arrive and almost immediately attacked him."

"There's nothing to show where the blows were struck? Blood spatter or pooling?"

"The first blow, no, but the blows that followed were inside the cottage. It isn't clear if he was attacked there or attacked as he opened the door and was then dragged inside and finished off. Forensics are still working on the evidence they took away, but I'm sure they'd have found something by now if there was anything to find."

"Well, here's my report," Pauline said. "I'm not sure it's any more hopeful than yours. The aging of the will as you know is in progress, but we won't have an answer for months, though that may not be a problem because the beneficiaries don't get anything until the tax man does and that can be up to six months. Anthony Thornton, however, is engaging a lawyer to challenge that because, he says, his father had changed the will in his favor."

"He never mentioned this before," Peacock said.

"No, it was a secret, he says. His father had suddenly come to the realization that progress must be made for the good of all and he thought Anthony the man to do that. He thought, so Anthony says, that Frank would just run the estate as it always has been run and he no longer believed that a good idea."

"And the old man didn't tell Frank or his lawyer, Ogilvie?"

"Anthony Thornton says his father told old Mr. Ogilvie but he's dead so we can't ask him. Presumably, Harry knew but he's dead too."

"May I say this is a very poor tale, Miss Riddell."

"But you have to admit, it's unassailable at this time. The only people who could refute it being dead."

"It also negates the aging test," Peacock said. "Obviously if the will was changed later, the sheets would be different ages."

"Yes," Pauline said. "Anthony is a sly customer. I almost admire him."

"What are your next steps? Do you even have any next steps?"

"I do but I'll wait to see if I can set up the series of events before I tell you what they are. And you two gentlemen, what are your next steps?"

"Steady police work, Miss Riddell, as always. We still have a long way to go before we make a breakthrough," Peacock said.

Pauline said nothing. Her mind was made up; the usual methods were not going to solve this case.

## 23

# SETTING A TRAP – JANUARY 10

PAULINE WATCHED Anthony Thornton mingle with the guests, noticing how he kept well away from her. It amused her for sooner or later, he must speak to her and that would be her time to put some pressure on him. From everything Frank Thornton had told her about his brother's mood, the strain of not getting the money was beginning to tell.

She saw her chance when he left the people he was talking to and headed to the drinks.

"Mr. Thornton," Pauline said, blocking his retreat from the side table where the punch bowl and other refreshments were placed, "I haven't had an opportunity to talk with you this evening and I've been so looking forward to doing that."

"I don't think you and I have anything to say to each other that would be important, Miss Riddell," he replied warily.

"Don't you?" She looked about in what she hoped was a nonchalant but obvious way, before continuing, "I'd like to tell you a story. It's about a man who wanted to defraud his brother and then had the plot run away from him and he ended up murdering people."

"It's sounds an exciting story, Miss Riddell. You should write it and find a publisher."

"In a way, that's what I plan to do. Only my publisher will be the police."

"And you think they will listen?"

"Yes, I do. You've been away from these parts for some years so you won't know it, but I have a reputation for getting these things right."

"So why tell me about it?"

"Because there's always the chance I may be wrong, so I want to give you a chance to say so before I bring us all into disrepute," Pauline said.

"If you think this man in your story is me, you're horribly wrong and you'll make yourself look ridiculous."

"Why don't we talk it over tomorrow, just the two of us, though I will have my brother close enough to see there's no violence," Pauline said. She stopped as a man came to the table to refill his and his partner's punch glasses. When he'd gone, she continued, "Shall we say eleven am tomorrow at the moor cross?"

"We'll freeze standing out there," Thornton said. The Moor Cross was an old stone cross, older than time, set up as a way marker where two drover roads, still visible in the landscape, crossed each other. It had a small parking area for it was a popular starting point for walkers in summertime.

"We won't be there long," Pauline said. "When you've heard what I have to say and given me some re-assurance of points that you'll say are untrue, we can quickly part as friends."

"And if I say no right now?"

"Then at eleven am tomorrow, I'll be talking to Inspector Peacock at Whitby Police Station. What I found among Walter's papers today will be enough to have you arrested."

Thornton frowned. "I've no idea what you're talking about. As I've told you before, you have it completely wrong, but I'll be there to see your evidence," he said and stalked off.

# 24

# LAYING THE BAIT – JANUARY 11

WHEN SHE SAW his car pull into the spot behind hers and him step out of the car she almost laughed. She wished she could have brought Sam Tunstall with her and he would have identified Thornton on the spot. The man's brown 'country' clothes stood out like a beacon, shouting 'London' or 'Paris' in this rural locality. She stepped out of her car to prevent him coming too close.

"I think we're close enough, Mr. Thornton," she said, as he continued to approach. "We can hear each other clearly from this distance."

"I don't want anyone overhearing your wild accusations," he said.

"Which is why I picked this lonely spot. However, just to be clear, if you look to your right, a way down the lane, you'll see my brother's Land Rover with him in it. He will watch what happens, though he can't hear what we're saying."

"What are we saying, Miss Riddell?"

"Let me tell you what I'm certain has happened here and give you some reasons why I believe I'm right. Then you can correct me if I've gone wrong in places, though I suspect, not far wrong."

"Tell your fiction, Miss Riddell, and I'll listen."

Pauline outlined how she thought events had played out and told him she had an eye witness who she was sure would identify him as being in contact with Walter. She had evidence that his wife had also been in contact with Walter, and she carried out the robberies, though Pauline was certain the woman would name him as being responsible for them. She told him how she had only suspicion until yesterday when, sorting through Walter's papers, she found a letter Walter had written in case anything should happen to him.

"You're just guessing Miss Riddell and you have no real proof. I don't think I'll say anything other than my wife has never left France and I only arrived in England in November. The police will soon show that to be true and your story nonsense."

Pauline nodded. "Very well," she said, turning towards her car.

"But," he said, "I don't need this bother right now so what can I offer, in the way of re-assurance, to make you go home and stop badgering me? I don't want to meet you again with things I think prove me innocent but that you won't accept."

"Proof you were elsewhere when my cousin was killed, would be a start," Pauline said. "After all, that's the most important thing to me and my family."

"And the rest?"

"As I said, my cousin is the most important thing. The rest, we can discuss."

"Then we can discuss now because I had no part in your cousin's death, Miss Riddell, nor did I kill Harry Clark so don't bother to continue down that path."

"The rest is only fraud," Pauline said, shrugging, "and none of it matters to me, except that justice should be done."

"Justice?" He snorted. "When has that ever been done?"

"As you say," Pauline remarked. "When. Take me, for

example. I've been solving crimes for the police and others for ten years now and I've grown tired of it. I'm vilified by the police and shunned by the very people who, I know, will come begging for my help if ever they need it. I charge a small fee. When I'm successful, they either refuse to pay or they pay only a fraction – claiming I'm only doing what any honest, civic-minded person would have done. The law is too blunt an instrument for justice. Only people can deliver that."

Thornton's expression remained bland, but Pauline could sense his excitement. He was wary but beginning to hope.

"I can appreciate everything you're saying, Miss Riddell," he said. "My brother, like our father before him, wants only to have the locals tugging their forelocks to him at church on Sunday. Whereas I see a great future here for me and the people of the estate if only we can unlock it, whenever I shared this with those two dinosaurs their opposition was unpleasant and they drove me out. Yes, I can understand the place you're reaching. I was there many years ago."

"And you believe your father's will is going to change that?"

"I do because over time, I was able to convince my father of the rightness of my cause. Frank's refusal to have the will made public convinces me my father did indeed change his will as he promised. I confess, I had little hope he'd done so until Frank began delaying."

"And you think the will gives you an opportunity to unlock the estate's potential?" Pauline asked, fascinated to hear what he would say. "He may only have made a more equitable sharing."

"My father wrote to me last year; we'd been in correspondence for some time, and assured me the estate was mine. He and I didn't get along and I couldn't help thinking he was playing an unkind trick on me for the way we've been to each other down the years."

He paused, and then continued, "As you can imagine, I'd hoped but didn't let my hopes grow too high because of our history together. I see now it must have been Frank he was playing a trick on for he didn't take my brother into his confidence."

"This seems a huge shift in your father's heart and mind," Pauline said.

Thornton nodded. "That's why I didn't believe at first but then his last letter to me said he'd finally come to understand I was right. The estate couldn't go on as it was – taxes alone would kill it – and progress demands we all move forward. He said he'd changed his will in my favor so I could lead the Thorntons forward and not stay stuck in an eighteenth-century rural rut."

"I see," Pauline said, "so that's what happened."

"You mean you know the will benefits me?"

Pauline shook her head. "Not as such," she said, "Like you, I just couldn't understand why your brother hadn't made it public already. You should understand many, my brother included, are in agony wondering about the future."

"Now you see why I'm so angry with Frank and why I'm taking legal advice," he said.

"I do see," Pauline said, thoughtfully. "And I share your belief in the future. All around us, we can see and feel change happening, politically, socially, in everything we hear on the radio or read in the papers. A radical departure from the past is upon us."

"Exactly," Thornton said, "and your brother and the other tenants need have no fear for the future. There will be better work for them than spending their lives out on the moors in all weathers. A new, brighter future beckons for all of us."

"And, in truth, I don't see why your plans for the estate and village are any worse than the static decay your brother's vision will bring about," Pauline said. "We've both been unappreciated by the world at large, Mr. Thornton, for just being ourselves. What you tell me gives me the courage to suggest how I could help bring that bright future about. I could be a fellow investor, a sleeping partner, if you like. It would have to be above-board, of course, legal and everything, just not public."

"I see you have the makings of a businesswoman as well as a detective," Thornton said. "Why don't I assemble the proof I need to show I didn't kill your cousin. I don't know how I might prove my innocence of Harry's death at present; it was so long ago. And then we meet here again tomorrow at this time. If my proof convinces you, then we can talk of partnerships."

"I agree," Pauline said. "Till tomorrow, then." She opened her car door and slipped quickly inside, closing and locking the door promptly. She needn't have done so for she could see in the rear-view mirror he was also back in his own car. The cold outside had been numbing, even, she thought, for sinners like Anthony Thornton who should already be feeling the heat of Hell beneath their feet.

Her route back to the farm took her past The Shepherd's Arms at lunch time and, at the side of the building, she saw Sam walking from his snowplow to the door of the pub. Pauline swerved into the parking lot, feeling the rear wheels slide on the hard-packed snow. The car slid to a halt between Sam and the door.

"What are you playing at," Sam said, rightly angry. "You could have killed me."

"Sorry," Pauline said. "I have a question I thought it best to ask away from the others."

He was immediately suspicious. "What is this question?"

"When you cut the grass around the radar domes, do you ever meet the people who work there?"

"People always ask that," he said. "They want to know if they look like James Bond."

"Well, do they?"

"I've never seen one person there, other than the man who opens and closes the gates for us and he's no James Bond. He's ninety if he's a day."

"You never see anyone?"

"Never, the others will tell you the same. We think the place may actually be run from elsewhere, only the radar equipment being there, like."

"How long have you worked there?"

"Two summers," Sam said. "We only do May to September."

"And you never see anyone or even any*thing*?"

Sam shook his head. "You'd expect it being summer, the workers would have their lunch outside to get some sun, like. Or there'd be cars or motorbikes parked. But no, nothing, not once in two years."

"Well, that's all I needed to know, thanks," Pauline said, winding up the window and backing away. Her theory about spying was a dead end. Sam said Walter was honest, and by his own rules she was pretty sure he was, and now this. No one had any opportunity to pass messages of any sort to Sam who would pass it to Walter and then him to a Russian captain. She could ask Sam's work colleagues, as he'd suggested, but he wouldn't have offered that if he didn't expect they'd give the same answer. They were probably all equally mystified by the golf balls, as everyone else was, even though they got up closer to them than anyone else. The only remaining lead was the one she'd just seeded. Would it grow?

# 25

# SATURDAY – JANUARY 11

SMOTHERED IN BLANKETS, with a rapidly cooling hot water bottle for company, Pauline lay uneasily in her bed. Her mind roamed unceasingly over the case and back across these past weeks, which was as well for she didn't want to sleep. Above all, she thought of Walter, as he was those years ago. Laughing, devil-may-care, always in some sort of minor trouble with everyone and always able to wheedle his way out of it. Tears pricked her eyes as she remembered that spring when she and Walter had wandered the moors together, looking for plover's eggs to sell to the gentry, or flint arrowheads to sell to the curio shops for visitors to buy. They'd fallen out when Walter showed her a pile of lead he'd 'acquired'. A scrap man would pay good money for it, better than eggs and Stone Age arrow-heads, he'd told her. But Pauline knew where the lead was from. The vicar of their church had told the congregation about a loss of lead sheet from the roof only the day before. Torn between her love and her duty, she'd fallen between the two. She parted from Walter, never speaking to him again, but didn't tell the adults what she knew. Compromise was the devil's work, as all her learning had taught her, and she swore she'd never do that again. She swore to herself that in her life, duty would always triumph.

Her thoughts strayed back and forth sadly until, just after one o'clock, when the wind's moaning around the chimney pots was growing into a banshee wail, she heard the faintest of clicks that sounded just like the old latch on the kitchen door.

She almost felt the cold draft from the opening and closing door, though she knew it was imagination brought on by hearing it blowing everything that was loose in the kitchen. Someone began climbing the stairs, stealthy footsteps that didn't know which steps creaked and which didn't. She could hear her parents breathing, her father's loud snores, her mother's softer ones. They didn't change their note. Before she left for home, she decided in that moment, she'd have all the door locks on this house changed. No one should be able to walk into a locked house this easily. The intruder listened at the head of the stairs before moving forward, the footsteps growing ever closer to Pauline's bedroom door. She sat up, placed pillows behind her back and braced herself against the bedhead.

The door opened and the intruder stopped, as Pauline switched on the bedside lamp.

"Good evening, Neville," she said. "This is very late for visiting."

The figure in the doorway was taken aback for a moment; dressed and groomed as Nicole, he expected to be unrecognized.

"Very clever," he said, in a soft feminine voice. "But Neville isn't here; I'm Nicole."

"You're here," Pauline said, "and that's all that matters. I've wanted to talk to you for some time now but you're hard to find."

"Not so hard, if you know where to look," he said, advancing from the door towards her.

"But I didn't know where to look."

"And now it's too late," he said. 'There's nothing more to be said."

"I hope you're at least going to tell me why you killed poor Walter," Pauline asked.

"Why should I?"

"Confession is good for the soul, they say," Pauline said, "but, if that isn't enough, tell me just to satisfy my curiosity and allow you to proclaim your triumph to someone. There will never be anyone else you can so safely tell."

He stopped, considering. "That's true," he said. "Tony doesn't like it anymore. Aging is a terrible thing; you lose your appetites, don't you find?"

"I'm not quite at an age where that is growing obvious," Pauline replied.

"If you had another ten years," he said, "you'd see. And to answer your question, I killed Walter because he called me names. It's as simple as that."

"He called you names," Pauline said, nodding. "I thought that might be it."

"They say 'sticks and stones may break my bones but names will never hurt me' but that's a lie, isn't it? It's the exact opposite of the truth. Don't you remember every horrible name you were called as a child and yet you can barely even remember broken bones?"

Pauline considered for a moment. "There's a lot of truth in that," she agreed. "And Harry?"

"Oh, that was just business. There was nothing personal, or pleasurable, in that."

"Which brings us to why you're here right now," Pauline said.

"It does," he agreed, "Except, I'm already enjoying you

trying to spin it out this way. It raises the anticipation wonderfully."

"If I call out, my father will be here in a moment."

"He's an old man," he said, "and will die right after you, as will your mother. If you care for them, you'll keep quiet."

"How can I be sure you won't kill them anyway, just for fun?" Pauline said.

"You can't, but I gave my word and that should be good enough for you." He drew out a long stiletto from his belt and took a step forward.

"You didn't believe my offer to go into business with you both?" Pauline asked, quickly.

Neville stopped. He shook his head. "No. Even if it was true, it cut the profits into three. That's too little reward."

"Does Anthony know you're here?" Pauline hoped to hear he did.

"No," Neville said, almost sadly, "he believes you. Thinks you're some sort of soulmate. Besides, like I said, he's grown old." Once again he took a step forward.

Pauline removed her hands from the blankets and pointed her automatic squarely at his face.

He stepped back.

"Drop the knife," Pauline said. When he didn't, she shifted her aim to his legs. "I won't tell you again," she said. "Drop the knife and we'll walk downstairs. You can leave without harm. Otherwise, you'll leave in an ambulance. I'm a good shot. I learned when I decided detecting crime was going to be my mission in life."

He dropped the knife and retreated to the door. In an instant, he'd leapt through it and slammed it shut.

Pauline smiled. The noise would be enough to awaken even the sleepiest of Peacock's men waiting in the living room below.

# 26

# CONCLUSION – SUNDAY MORNING, JANUARY 12

"THAT'S ALL VERY WELL, POLLY," Alan said. "But why did you think Tony Thornton was behind everything?"

"Other than him being a thoroughly bad lot, you mean," Pauline said.

"Alan's point is a fair one, though, Pauline," her mother said. "Just because someone isn't a nice person, you can't just suspect them of being forgers and murdering people, especially when they weren't even in the country at the time."

"I think we all understood he had to be behind the forged will," Pauline said. "It was the only thing that made sense. He wrote that nasty note suggesting he didn't know but it couldn't overcome the obvious and I don't really think it fooled anyone. The difficulty was seeing how those unpleasant incidents and break-ins were related and then seeing how any of that related to Walter's death."

Alan sighed and rolled his eyes. "That's what I asked you, Polly," he said. "Stop being annoying and tell us why or how you made the connection."

"Inspector Peacock helped me a lot there," she replied. "Anthony Thornton gambled a lot and he lost a lot. In particular, they heard he'd lost heavily at a private club on his first day back in London, which was in mid-November."

"How does that affect anything here?" her father asked. "Nobody here even knew he was in the country so what does it mean?"

"Somebody here was affected," Pauline said. "The Frenchwoman staying at the Dower house."

"So, she was his wife," her mother said. "Our suspicions were right all along."

"In a manner of speaking," Pauline said. "Anyway, up till then she'd been getting by on the money he sent her. Now, she was told there was no more coming. It was probably intended to be a temporary setback. After all, it likely happened often enough. Anyway, it meant a change in her activities. No more revenge attacks; now they had to be focused on getting money."

"When I said that haul of silver could be carried by one person," Inspector Peacock interjected, "I should have said but not likely by a woman."

"Quite so," Pauline said. "It was the same with Walter's body. A man may carry him some distance, but a woman was unlikely. She'd have to be one of those Soviet weightlifters. But a man who passed himself off as a woman, could easily have done both."

"Walter saw her when she was out at night, when he was out at night," Peacock said.

Pauline nodded. "And thought he'd make some money for himself by offering to fence the loot. I don't know if Walter recognized her immediately or something he saw or heard alerted him, but he knew who she was."

"Neville Duck," her mother said.

"Yes, exactly. Neville left the village years ago, right after Anthony himself. I guess it was planned. Anyhow, he made his way to Anthony Thornton's house in the south of France.

Then he disappeared, only to re-emerge as a 'woman refugee' from the North African independence wars. They married and lived quietly down there, or at least that's what Anthony told everyone. There doesn't seem to have been a legal ceremony either here in England or in France."

"Which is why Anthony partied so hard when he came to England, I guess," Peacock said. "He couldn't rock the boat in France, but he could go overboard here, in a private sort of way."

"I think so," Pauline said. "I don't think he was the sort of person that could deny his nature for long."

"What do you think Neville Duck thought about it? He can't have been pleased, stuck down in the French home, living quietly, while his partner was off making a splash in London or even around here once in a while."

"I suspect he traveled here too," Pauline said. "He would still have his Neville Duck papers in addition to his Nicole Dubois papers. Provided he never came here as Neville Duck, no one would know or care who he was."

"Was it Neville or Nicole that killed Walter, do you think?" her father asked.

"It's hard to know but I suspect Walter had already guessed and begun his blackmail effort so it would probably be as Neville that the murderer arrived at the house that night. Walter opened the door, thinking it was his friend Sam, and was struck almost immediately with a metal bar. The first blow stunned him, as the pathologist said. The second and third killed him."

"Then quickly out onto the moors with the body," Peacock said.

"Yes," Pauline replied. "If the weather had been better, I imagine he'd have taken more time to hide it, but the snow made all that useless anyhow. Unless it snowed so hard the tracks he was leaving carrying the body out there were completely covered, the body was going to be quickly found."

"But, Pauline," her mother said. "Nicole had left the neighborhood at least two weeks before. I remember Mrs. Drayton telling me and that was when I was buying overseas stamps for Christmas cards."

"It looked that way to everyone," Pauline agreed, "and it was an easy fiction to maintain, until the snow came. The snow made it hard for him to get in and out of the house without leaving tracks. The weather turning like it did was pure bad luck for them."

"You say for 'them' but I still don't see the connection to Anthony. Why was Duck here at all?"

"Frank Thornton wrote his brother a letter saying their father was dying and Anthony should come back to be with him at the end. I think that set in motion a long-standing plan which had been waiting years to come to fruition. Five years or so before, Anthony had made Harry Clark change the Thornton will. He may have bribed him or blackmailed him; we can't know for sure. Anthony knew no one would spot the change until his father died, or at least was dying, because no one does check these things, certainly not in old families like the Thorntons and the Ogilvies. When he learned his father was dying, he sent Neville in his guise as Nicole to the Dower house to watch and relay back information."

"This being the first time he'd been back in the village since before the War," Peacock added, "he couldn't resist acting out some reprisals on those he felt had picked on him as a child."

'But poor Miss Goforth never hurt anyone!" her father exclaimed. "She was the gentlest of creatures."

"Unfortunately, some people can't resist hurting those who they know won't hurt them back," Pauline said. "Miss Goforth always had a cat and Neville liked to hurt small animals. I've no doubt on at least one occasion, she was roused to the defense of her pet and young Neville was punished for it."

"It's true what you say," Alan agreed. "He did like hurting animals, everything from butterflies to cats, even small dogs, I remember it was said, though no one proved anything."

"And Tom Pringle was often at Neville's father's cottage about various allegations from angry pet owners," her father added.

"Neville hasn't lost his taste for cruelty, even now," Mrs. Riddell said.

"It seems not," Peacock added. "The St. Tropez gendarmerie have a catalogue of incidents going back years. They may now be able to clear that up."

"If he isn't hanged for Walter's murder," Mr. Riddell said.

"I hope he is," Pauline said. "Cruelty to animals ranks high on my list of capital offenses. Even farmers and slaughterhouses do what they can to kill their animals humanely. People like Neville Duck kill for pleasure and take pleasure in doing it in the cruelest way they can."

"I'm not sure the rest of us are ready to elevate cruelty to animals to a capital offense though, Miss Riddell," Peacock said, grinning.

"Well, you should be. In my experience most animals are decent human beings and too many human beings aren't even decent animals, so I think it's time for us to reconsider," Pauline said. "However, in this case, it is a moot point. He killed at least one human being in cold blood and that should be enough."

"Anthony Thornton may yet escape though," Peacock said. "It's hard to show he ordered the killing. He claims he was as horrified as we are at what was done. All we have on him is accessory to murder because he drove Duck to

Walter's house and then drove him away. We also have receiving stolen goods and selling them on."

"I wish you'd been able to get better prints from the crime scene, Inspector. It might have shown which one carried the body out."

"*Our* best hope is to get Duck to understand *his* best hope is to accuse Thornton, instead of accepting the present state of affairs."

"You must show him he'll definitely hang if he doesn't," Pauline said.

"We have tried, Miss Riddell, but I fear the man really does love Thornton and remains faithful to the end. It's hard to imagine murderers and torturers having such feelings but there you are. We all have some spark of humanity, it seems."

"But the will, dear. How did you guess that?" her mother asked.

"In some ways, that was the easiest part. I was talking all this over with you and Dad. Dad told me of Harry's sister. He was the one who gave me the information I needed."

"But I didn't really know that I was being such a help," her father said, laughing.

"I didn't really know then either," Pauline said, "but I was sure Harry would have kept that page as insurance. I'm sure he would know how dangerous it could be for him if the forgery was discovered and he was suspected. Going to Spain kept him out of the police's reach but not that of Anthony Thornton, or worse, Neville Duck."

"We'd searched for it," Peacock said. "It wasn't among the papers Harry left to his cousin and his house in Spain was ransacked. By the time we realized there might be a missing page, it had been emptied ready for sale. We didn't know if it was there or had been found. We thought we had to give up."

"I thought so too," Pauline said. "After all, if they'd found it, they would have destroyed it. But the more I thought about it the less likely that seemed. I put myself in the shoes of someone who has an insurance policy against dangerous criminals. Where would I hide it? Not on my person, they'd look there first. Not in my house, they'd search that next. Maybe with a lawyer? In the bank? But this 'insurance' is criminal so maybe not those places. I was pondering all this when Dad telling me about Walter's sister came back into my head. I looked up when she died, and learned it was in the year before Harry retired."

"I could have told you that too, if you'd asked," her father said.

"But when you first told me, I hadn't seen the connection. It was later I had the idea it may mean something."

"Now I think on it myself," her father said, "I should have realized too, for Harry talked to no one except his sister and that's who he'd take it to for safekeeping. He was an odd man in many ways."

"Until Dad told me, nobody had mentioned Harry having a sister," Pauline said. "I asked Dad why no one had mentioned her before."

He nodded. "I told Pauline, 'She's dead. She died in '57'. I remember Harry was devastated. He and his sister had lived in that house since their parents died nearly twenty years before."

"We don't know for sure when the forgery was made," Pauline said, "but it must have been around that time. In fact, I think it was the death of his sister that finally made Harry agree to Anthony Thornton's plan. He wanted to get away."

"I have to admit," Peacock said, "when Miss Riddell came to me with her idea, I was extremely skeptical. But when she explained that Harry's sister was buried in the churchyard at about the time the forgery was almost certainly made and maybe Harry thought putting the page in with her, or at least in beside the coffin, as a safe place, I could see we

162

had to investigate. The cousin was agreeable, so we had the exhumation order in record time, thanks to having a local Justice of the Peace, Mr. Frank Thornton, on our side."

"Thankfully," Pauline said, "it was in a box on top of the coffin and we didn't need to disturb the body at all."

"Gives you another charge against Thornton, doesn't it, Inspector?" Alan asked. "Forgery?"

"Anthony Thornton maintains there is no forgery, as you'd expect, and the aging tests are months away from being finished. Even then, it will likely only be 'this page is aged differently' rather than a date when it was typed," Peacock said. "It may be difficult to find the evidence to press charges. We all know he orchestrated the affair, but Harry typed and switched the pages. We no longer have his bank accounts to see if he was paid for it and by who. I feel we may not be able to make a charge stick."

"As Shakespeare said, 'all's well that ends well'," Mrs. Riddell said. "I think this has ended well and, even better, Pauline still has a half day left of her holidays."

Pauline laughed. "It's been quite a break," she said. "Mum being ill, the worst weather since I don't know when and worst of all, a murder."

"Will you come to Walter's funeral, Pauline?" her mother asked. "Now the body is to be released, we can get it arranged."

Pauline hesitated. She'd thought about this during her long vigil of the night and decided. "I'll be too busy, Mum," she said.

"They must have compassionate leave where you work," her father protested.

"For close relatives," Pauline said, "they do. Not a cousin though. And I think I prefer to remember Walter as he was when I knew him, not as he became."

"You and he were thick as thieves once," her brother said.

"Yes," Pauline agreed, "we were and maybe if we'd stayed so, he could have been kept from the life he lived since. Unfortunately, I fear, I would have followed him and not the other way around. I think it best we continue to go our separate ways."

Her father nodded solemnly. "Walter was always full of surprises and his murder was his last, though it wasn't of his doing."

"It was his final gift to me," Pauline said, "a murder for Christmas." Her voice was steady, but her heart ached for that foolish young boy and girl all those years ago.

# POLITE REQUEST

THANK you for reading my book. If you love this book, please, please don't forget to leave a review on Amazon! Every review matters and it matters a lot for independent authors!

I'll make it super-easy to do that on Amazon by placing the link here:

A Murder for Christmas

And THANK YOU now and forever if you do:-)

# BONUS CONTENT

Here's an excerpt from my next book in the series, *Miss Riddell and the Heiress:*

**Sydney, NSW, Australia, November, 1977**

Pauline broke off a piece of her Lamington cake and watched the woman approach. The woman had been on the morning Captain Cook Cruise around the harbor and bay that Pauline had taken and she'd seemed to take a special interest in Pauline. Pauline wracked her brain to make a connection between the woman and the many new people she'd met since arriving in Australia only four weeks earlier. She couldn't think of anyone she'd met that fitted the woman, who was circling closer, unable to decide whether to speak or leave.

The woman was dressed for a vacation and that alone set her apart from the other Australians all around who were in 'winter' clothes, this being the depths of Sydney's winter season. Pauline was in her spring clothes for to a northern Englishwoman, an Australian winter was more like a summer's day. But this mysterious, and conflicted stranger, was also in her summery clothes of flower-printed dress and bare legs, though with a light, fawn coat over her arm.

Pauline took a sip of tea and continued nibbling her cake while she waited for the woman to make up her mind. Lamington cake, a sponge cube rolled in chocolate and shredded coconut, was interesting but, in the end, just sponge cake. In Pauline's mind, pastries were always better than cakes. The zoo café was busy with families enjoying snacks in the bright sunshine and under the clear blue sky that hadn't changed since she'd arrived in Australia. Those crowds, however, made it hard for Pauline to always keep the woman in sight.

She was an attractive woman who, somewhat unusually, wore no jewelry to enhance her face, neck or arms. Her honey-blonde hair was fashionably cut but not in the hideous modern styles that came from watching too much television or the movies. Pauline guessed she was about thirty, though her manner was almost that of a socially awkward teenager. Her hovering wasn't threatening but even if it had been, Pauline wouldn't have been concerned. They were evenly matched in height and weight and Pauline, when the dangers of her forays into crime solving had become too apparent, had taken lessons in self defense. She saw herself very much in the mould of Mrs. Emma Peel in the silly television show, The Avengers, that had been so popular in the Sixties. Though she fully recognized, and disapproved of, the nonsense it showed, she'd taken lessons nevertheless. While she knew even a trained woman like herself couldn't win a fight against a violent, aggressive man, let alone the kind of supposedly trained agents Mrs. Peel was always besting in fights, it was enough to know that the element of surprise early in a fight could turn out in her favor.

Just as Pauline was thinking of leaving the small table, the woman came to a decision and approached her directly.

"Excuse me," she said. "Can I talk to you for a moment?"

She spoke English with an Australian accent, Pauline noticed, not Australian English. Perhaps she was a newcomer who was just beginning to settle in.

"Of course," Pauline said, gesturing to the seat at the opposite side of the small table.

"You don't know me," the woman said, abruptly, and stopped.

"Well, we can correct that at once," Pauline said. "I'm Pauline Riddell." She held out her hand.

The woman took Pauline's hand and shook it. Her hand was soft but her handshake firm. Despite her initial suspicions, Pauline felt herself thawing.

"Alexandra Wade," she said, "but I prefer just plain, Alex." She stopped speaking abruptly again but this time it seemed less odd because she was settling herself in the chair Pauline had offered.

Pauline decided to wait it out. The woman wanted to talk, that was clear but she'd have to decide to do so in her own time. After all, Pauline was flying home tomorrow and couldn't help anyone here. She mentally shook herself. No one here knew she was Miss Riddell, fighter for justice and righter of wrongs, as her journalist friend Poppy had once described her in a newspaper article. She smiled to herself. Poppy's words from long ago and far away, while silly, did come to mind often, which was of course pride and a failing she did her best to suppress.

"You talked about Whalley to the people on the boat this morning," Alexandra said, at last.

For a moment, Pauline had a mental block, then remembered, "Oh, yes," she said, "the British couple on the boat told me they were from Manchester before emigrating here. They asked me if I knew Manchester."

Alexandra nodded. "Then you said you lived in Whalley."

"I do," Pauline said. "I moved there some months ago. Why, do you know it?"

"I've never been there but I know of it," Alex said. "My Mum said we were descendants of a noble family from near there." She paused, then continued. "Do you know a village called Ashton de Cheney?"

"No," Pauline said slowly, "but I'm not a local in the area. As I said, I only moved there a few months ago. Do you live in Sydney? It's a beautiful city."

"No," Alex said, "I come from Victoria. Wadeville, it's a tiny place about a hundred miles inland from Melbourne."

"I've heard Melbourne is a beautiful city too," Pauline said.

"I wouldn't know," Alex said, "apart from the airport, I've never been there."

"Never?" Pauline asked.

"We never got off the station much when I was a kid," Alex said, "then when Dad took off, and we lost the farm and had to move into town, Mum and me couldn't afford to go anywhere."

"I'm sorry," Pauline said. "Still, the country around there must be beautiful so you can't have missed much growing up."

"It is pretty around there," Alex agreed. "Living there, you forget. It takes a stranger to remind you of things sometimes."

"That's very true," Pauline said. "Visitors come to where I grew up all the time and it was a long time before I could see the moors as they saw them."

"My difficulty is different." Alex said. "The country I grew up in is beautiful but our poverty, after Dad left, makes me hate it."

"I'm sorry to hear that," Pauline said, though wondering

what any of this had to do with her. "It must have been very hard."

Alex shook her head. "You don't understand, I'm not explaining it well. It was a poverty of mind as well as body, and it was made worse by my mother's belief we were 'Quality', as she called it, and we had to keep ourselves above our neighbors."

Pauline was beginning to think the woman wasn't quite right in the head and considered how best to extricate herself from this increasingly worrisome interview.

"It is hard when you're young to not have things others have," Pauline said.

"It wasn't like that," Alex said, almost angrily. "I didn't care about material things. It was the lack of friends, the loneliness, the teasing and bullying at school that drove me to leave school early and miss out on college."

Pauline frowned. Any moment, she'd be asked to donate to something, she was sure of it.

Seeing Pauline's expression seemed to sober Alex and she said, "You see, I lived all my life in a tiny village of fifty people and hadn't a relative or friend in the whole place. My mother's obsession with being 'aristocracy' kept us apart. People don't like being told they're below you on some idiotic social scale from a far-away country."

"I can see how that would cause friction," Pauline agreed, and she could. The woman's mother must have been deranged to give herself airs and graces in a land as egalitarian as Australia prided itself on being.

"Friction doesn't begin to describe it," Alex said, her temper clearly rising again. "When I was a teenager, the other kids were always having crushes on each other, going out, falling out. Nobody wanted me. Mother would say 'a pretty girl like you will soon get a good husband, not one of these local yokels' but she didn't have to run home from school to stop the yokels pawing her, not because they were attracted to me but because they wanted to hurt and humiliate me. Mother's obsession was a nightmare I lived with until..." she stopped.

"Until?" Pauline said, feeling the woman was getting to the point at last.

"She died, about a month ago."

"Oh, I am sorry," Pauline said. Did the woman just want a shoulder to cry on? Pauline hoped not for she wasn't the shoulder-crying-on sort.

The silence grew as Alex clearly tried to recover her thoughts and feelings.

"I have no one, you see, or not really," she said, at last, "and I don't like where I live so I thought I'd make the trip to England to see if what mother said was true."

"I still don't understand why you're telling me this or what it is you hope to learn in England," Pauline said.

"Mother said I'm the rightful heir to the de Cheney estate in a village called Ashton de Cheney and one day we'd go back and claim it."

Pauline asked, "Was your mother from Ashton de Cheney?"

Alex shook her head. "No," she said. "It was my real Dad who was the de Cheney. Mum was just a regular girl. They met in the war but he was killed before I was even born. And so were his parents, by a bomber unloading its bombs. Mum said the Jerry was afraid of all the flak over Liverpool so he dropped his bombs early and scampered back to Germany. She says it happened a lot. The Jerries were cowardly like that, not like our boys who flew right into the thick of it." She paused, then added, "My real father was a bomber pilot and he was killed over Germany. That may have clouded her judgment."

172

Pauline smiled; Alex's wryly honest comment confirmed what she'd suspected. Beneath that awkward manner was a more mature woman trying to emerge.

"Perhaps," Pauline said, 'but still I prefer simple national pride to the modern fashion for revisionism."

"I do too," Alex said, "I feel the pilots on both sides were incredibly brave though I never told mother that. She'd have skinned me alive."

"It's always a mistake to run down your enemy," Pauline agreed. "It devalues your victory if you win and humiliates you further if you lose."

"Exactly," Alex said.

"I still don't see why you wanted to speak to me?" Pauline asked. She felt it was time to get to the heart of the issue before her whole afternoon was lost.

"If I'm the rightful heir to the de Cheney estate, or at least I have a claim on it," Alex said, "I'd like to know. Some money would be welcome, of course, though I've a good job now so it isn't just that. It's that I may have a family who may even be happy to know me."

This story was different, Pauline thought. Since arriving in Australia she'd heard one or two strange stories about 'back home' but this one was unusual. A missing heiress was straight out of romance novel, and it quite likely was!

"So why didn't your mother claim the estate for you?" she asked. "After all, the postal service is very quick and efficient nowadays."

"Because her husband died before his parents did and he never got to pass it on to her," Alex replied. "Presumably the inheritance passed to some other branch of the family."

"That's bad luck," Pauline agreed.

"I think so," Alex said seriously, "but I imagine it happened a lot in history. All those wars and plagues and things."

"Probably it did," Pauline agreed again.

"What would happen if there wasn't another branch of the family?"

"I'm not a lawyer," Pauline said, "and I'm sure it depends on the circumstances but I'd guess it goes to the State."

"What if someone claimed it years later?"

"I've no idea," Pauline said. "Probably a successful claimant would inherit but, again I'm guessing, there must be a time period allowed. You couldn't claim too long after the death or the State would have disposed of it. Are you thinking you might have a case?"

"Lately," Alex said slowly, "I've been wondering. Since Mum died I've been on my own and I thought a trip to England might... you know. Well, you wouldn't because I don't know..." Alex let the sentence dribble away into nothing.

"I'm sorry I can't be more help," Pauline said. 'I really know very little about inheritance law." This wasn't entirely truthful but Pauline didn't want to give the woman false hopes. She saw Alex nod in thanks but her mind was far away.

"I do hope you're able to get the help you need," Pauline began, gathering her purse and jacket in preparation for leaving.

"Please," Alex said, "don't go. I only want to know something of where you live and how I might begin my quest for the truth. Just a few minutes, please?"

Pauline laid her bag and jacket down. It was difficult. She was torn between her usual desire to help others who needed help and her equally strong desire to not be imposed upon.

"Tell me quickly what you want to know," Pauline said, "and I'll do my best."

"Where is the village? I couldn't find it on the map?"

"I'm as puzzled about that as you are," Pauline said. "I've never heard of it and yet you think it's somewhere near where I live."

"Well where is that?"

"In Lancashire, just a few miles north of Manchester," Pauline said.

"So, I could fly to London and then take a train to there?"

"Yes, very easily."

"How would I find out about wills and family matters?"

"Do that at Somerset House in London before you travel north," Pauline said, happier now they were talking practical matters.

"As easy as that?"

"Research is never quite that easy but that's where you start," Pauline said.

"Thank you," Alex said, "I had no idea. Could I ask a favor? It won't take much of your time."

"If I can," Pauline said, wary again.

"If I give you my address would you find out what you can about the village and hall of Ashton de Cheney and send me the details? That way I'd know if there even is such a place because from what you've said, and my map reading, there isn't."

"Yes, I think I could do that," Pauline said, making a mental note not to provide a return address on her letter. "It should be a quick and simple history project and I liked doing those at school."

"I always hated history," Alex said. "My life was blighted by history and I couldn't see how it might help anyone to know more of it."

Pauline smiled. "Well, this time it might work out to your benefit. If I find there isn't or wasn't an Ashton de Cheney, you'll be saved the expense of the trip and if I find there was, you may have the opportunity of a family and some additional money. A win-win as we say in business."

If this extract has whetted your appetite to read more, you can pre-order the book here.

# DEDICATION

*For my family. The inspiration they provide and the time they allow me for imagining and typing makes everything possible.*
*I'd also like to thank my editors, illustrator and the many others who have helped with this book. You know who you are.*

# COPYRIGHT

Even More Information

Email pj4429358@gmail.com

Twitter: https://twitter.com/pauljames953

Facebook: https://www.facebook.com/pauljamesauthor

Facebook: https://www.facebook.com/
PCJamesAuthor/MissRiddellCozyMysteries

❀ Created with Vellum

# MORE OF MY BOOKS

You can find more books by P.C. James and Paul James here:

P.C. James Author Page: https://www.amazon.com/P.-C.-James/e/B08VTN7Z8Y

Paul James Author Page: https://www.amazon.com/-/e/B01DFGG2U2

GoodReads: https://www.goodreads.com/author/show/20856827.P_C_James

# NEWSLETTER

To be kept up-to-date on everything in the world of Miss Riddell Cozy Mysteries, sign up to my Newsletter here.

# ABOUT THE AUTHOR

I've always loved mysteries, especially thosc involving Agatha Christie's Miss Marple. Perhaps because Miss Marple reminded me of my aunts when I was growing up. But Agatha Christie never told us much about Miss Marple's earlier life. When writing my own elderly super-sleuth series, I'm tracing her career from the start -- as you'll see if you follow the Miss Riddell Cozy Mysteries over the coming years.

However, this is my Bio, not Miss Riddell's, so here goes with all you need to know about me:

I'm a retired manager and a budding writer. When I'm not staring at the computer screen in the hope inspiration will strike, you'll find me running, walking, and taking wildlife photographs around Whitby, Ontario, Canada. My series begins in northern England because that was my home growing up and England is also the home of so many great cozy mysteries. Stay with me though because the Miss Riddell stories will take us to many different places around the world.

Printed in Great Britain
by Amazon